Enter In

Connie Ann DeVanna-Francis

ISBN 978-1-0980-3887-8 (paperback)
ISBN 978-1-0980-3888-5 (digital)

Christian Faith Publishing, Inc.
832 Park Avenue
Meadville, PA 16335
www.christianfaithpublishing.com

Printed in the United States of America

CONTENTS

In the beginning was the **Word**, and the Word was with God, and the Word was God.

—John 1:1

For the WORD of God is quick, and powerful, and sharper than any two edged sword, piercing even to the dividing asunder of the soul and spirit, and the joints and marrow, and is a discerner of the thoughts and intents of the heart.

—Hebrews 4:12

For thou wilt light my candle: the Lord my God will enlighten my darkness.

—Psalms 8:28

No man, when he hath lighted a candle, covereth it with a vessel, or putteth it under a bed; but setteth it on a candlestick, that they which **enter in** may see the light.

—Luke 8:16

PREMISE

The past is done and over with and impossible to change, but Matthew Thomas, a middle-aged man, is stuck somewhere in his childhood. He carries a scar from his youth that has physically healed but still pulsates with pain on his soul and motivates his self-will for vengeance, yet he has become passive and numb for one reason or another. What if he could do something to relieve the trauma, shame, and guilt of the secrets that long for vengeance? Especially the verbal and/or a physical abuse by someone who should have been protecting him, or the dagger of betrayal that almost severed his heart from his chest in his adult life? Matthew's secrets and bad memories are buried deep in the recesses of his mind and heart. But they badger and continue to scream their taunts that no one else hears, but himself. Yet he continues to deny, hide, bury the guilt, and shame while resurrecting phony headstones in his heart that say, RIP!

Matthew Thomas works for an alarm company as one of their best technicians, specializing in installing, inspecting, troubleshooting, and reactivating security systems that have been out of service. Matthew's job is to make sure that all the sensors are communicating and transferring properly from the systems control to the monitoring center.

At the risk of depression and stuck in his pain, Matthew uses alcohol to escape his past and to help silence the voices that are recorded in the parched wells in his soul, to try to bring temporary relief to his mourning. He has grown callous to his own God-given internal alarm signals that have been chewed, gnawed, blocked, and severed by the toxic echoes of his dysfunctional childhood memories of his abusive father and abused mother. Matthew and his sisters knew nothing else but this way of life but dream and hoped for something better.

Miss prim and proper, goody two shoes, Phyllis Jones, is the nosy neighbor who lived across the street from Matthew when he was a child. Her so-called "religion" was and is the only cover for hiding her own toxic secrets. She is the mother of Daniel Jones, a childhood classmate "bully," also employed at the same alarm company, which makes the ever present reminder and pain in Matthew's backside ongoing.

Due to an unexpected accident, Matthew is called to cover part of Daniel's scheduled work orders and ends up doing a service call at the address of his childhood home. Upset beyond measure and trying his best to get out of doing it, but to no avail, Matthew has to follow through as scheduled.

This encounter causes deeply buried memories to bubble back up to the surface of Matthew's heart and causes him to reflect on the place of his suffering. But during this work order to his childhood home, Matthew finds a major puzzle piece to his father's anger and rage, tucked away in the attic, as he ran wires for additional protection for the current owner.

This flashback event causes Matthew to go back to another location that silently beckons for his return. This property, now in ruins, Matthew tries to find clues that started the chain reaction to that traumatic summer. In this former summer camp of foundational building of character, Matthew is drinking heavily to try and forget 1966, the worst summer of his life. Matthew ends up sending out test signals to the Master of the universe and to his surprise, it causes him to encounter a wonderful mysterious "tree of life" of an unknown city of bees.

As Matthew enters in to this tree of life, he ends up taking a trip into the core of his soul, to ride his "train of thought" to places that he is in denial that exist within him. If a picture is worth a thousand words, so much more are the pictures inside Matthew's dark forest of his past and the required courage to see the internal battle of self-will, which left unchecked, can leave the soul imprisoned.

During this unexpected trip to the core of his being and the land of his heart, Matthew encounters, not only his secrets, but is lead to his pain to find where his treasure is and his greatest enemy to himself, and he discovers a key answer to win the battle from the inside out.

So come, enter in and take an unusual exploration trip into someone's thoughts and heart to reveal the absolute simplicity that only the *word* can reveal. We all have dark places, but the beauty is in that our maker knows all these things and has promised so much more if only we learn to look inward.

So the question is, will you *enter in*? RIP—real inner peace!

CHAPTER 1
The Injustice of 1966

On a warm summer afternoon in 1966, a sliver haired frail man named Jack Thomas laid down his pen on his desk and pushed a piece of paper aside. Slowly, he brought his hands to his face to wipe the tears that started to run, and at that moment, a bright shaft of light entered from his cell window. Jack turned his head slightly and smiled as if he were greeting a secret friend of the past few years. He lifted his hand as a sign of welcome and wiggled his fingers through the beam of light to stir the dust particles, then watched them dance about as the sunlight caused them to appear as tiny twinkling flares. They looked like innumerable minute cells, moving under a microscope, and it gave every impression this light source was fully alive!

Jack enjoyed these visits that came from the heavens. They were special and very personal to him and never lasted as long as he would have liked, but today, it came at a moment that he really needed it. Jack closed his eyes as the light touched upon his face; he began soaking in the warmth, comfort, peace, and love.

Every deep line on his face seemed to relax and melt, a glimmer of hope showed up, and Jack embraced faith once again. It was as if liquid light entered every pore of his exposed skin and ran deep, deep into the core of his being to water the soil of his soul. No one could steal this from him. Jack was resting in green pastures even though his flesh was locked away. After a few moments of private, intimate, spiritual, and soulful fellowship, the brilliance of its essence, that so gently entered, started to fade and exit with the same overwhelming grace.

Jack picked his pen back up and continued to finish a letter he had started. About an hour later, he heard the wheels of the mail cart coming his way. "Hey, Jack, any out going mail today?" the guard asked.

"Yes, yes I do. Did I get any mail?" Jack said as he slid the envelope through the bars of his cell.

"Sorry Jack not today!" the guard stated, as he took the letter and put it in the outgoing mailbag. The motion of the cart was already moving for the next cell, and the guard was gone.

That same afternoon of 1966

The gentle ripples and reflections of sparkling diamonds were dancing on the surface of the water at the public pool when ten-year-old Daniel Jones did a cannon ball with well-calculated precision. It was like watching this event in s-l-o-w motion, every drop of water hit its intended target of sunbathers on the edge of the pool, including a few women that appeared to have come straight from the beauty parlor.

Attitudes were erupting from all directions from this inconsiderate prank. One young momma, who was standing waist high in the water, along with her now screaming three month old, turned around with her now crooked sunglasses, half soaked hair, and one huge black smudge running down her face from her non-waterproof mascara yelled, "You jerk!"

Daniel had just resurfaced from the deep and shrugged his shoulders with a pathetic acknowledgment that he had anything to do with the surprise soaker. A ten-year-old black boy named Marcus was in the shallow end of the pool, feeling the wake of Daniel's cannon ball. Daniel wiped the water from his eyes and set his sights on his next victim.

Just outside the gate of the pool, Matthew Thomas (also ten years) and his two older sisters, Millie and Betty, parked their bikes and raced to the pool to see who could get there first. Matthew reached the gate first, entered, and ran to the nearest bench to drop off his towel so he could start scanning the pool to see who all was there. He spotted Daniel, his neighbor, and classmate, reeling in his next prey.

Like a crocodile, Daniel slithered in the water up to the black boy. "Hey, are you new around here?"

Marcus seemed shocked yet excited that someone even noticed him and answered awkwardly, "Yeah, I just moved here a couple weeks ago."

Daniel, still hovering with his face partially in the water, said, "Do you want to help me find my quarter? I think it fell out of my bathing suit pocket."

Marcus looked concerned, "Where do you think you lost it?"

Daniel pointed a little beyond the rope that divided the shallow from the deep end of the pool, "Somewhere down there I think!"

Not wanting to say that he really couldn't swim, Marcus walked deeper into the pool till he could touch the floating rope. He lifted it over his head so he would be on the deeper side, but he was still able to touch the bottom with his toes. Daniel continued wooing him, "If you help me find it, I will share a snack with you from the concession stand."

"Oh, okay!" Marcus agreed. He pinched his nose and went under water but lost his grip of the rope.

Daniel went in for the score, he descended under the water to locate where Marcus was and then shoved him out further into the deep. Marcus was out of breath and headed for the surface but could no longer touch the bottom. Marcus had trouble staying afloat. Matthew was already running to the pool to help out this poor soul because he knew first hand how this bully operated. Daniel was already out of sight, hiding in a crowd of swimmers in the deep end.

Marcus was gasping for air and was in a full-blown panic. Matthew jumped in the pool as close to the black boy as he could get and pulled him to the floating rope where he could touch the bottom once again. Marcus was coughing and trying his hardest not to cry. "Thanks," Marcus said, clearing his throat.

Matthew placed his hand on his shoulder, "No problem! Daniel does this stuff all the time! You really can't trust him ever!" Matthew graced him a moment to gather himself. "I'm Matthew!"

Marcus was still struggling not to cry. "Thanks Matthew! I'm Marcus. I moved here just a couple of weeks ago."

They both got out of the water and headed to the playground area, which was almost empty that afternoon. These two became best buds before they were even dry from the water fiasco. Matthew said, "Hey, you want to come to my house? I don't live far from here and we can get away from this snake?"

Marcus lit up, "Sure, let's go. I don't have to be home till four."

Matthew said, "I will go let my sisters know I am leaving." Proudly, he added, "I want you to meet my mom!"

Marcus was walking by Matthew as he pushed his bike down the sidewalk toward Matthew's house. Matthew asked, "Where do you live?"

"I live right down this road, just over the railroad tracks."

"Wow, that's really close to my house! There is only one bad thing though, Daniel lives right across the street from me," Matthew stated while rolling his eyes.

The boys were coming up to the house, and Bruce (Matthew's dad) was bent over working under the hood of the car. Timidly, Matthew said, "Dad?"

Bruce answered sternly, "What do you want?"

"Is mom home?"

Still under the hood of the car, his dad echoed, "She's at the store."

With a huge disappointed expression, Matthew looked at Marcus, "Okay."

Bruce took one step back from the car and peeked over the top of his reflective sunglasses, which you could see both of the boys images mirrored in the lenses. Bruce took one look at this black boy and fired back loudly, "Matthew, get in the house now!"

Inside the house across the street, Phyllis Jones (Daniel's mom) pulled back her lace curtain, straining to hear and get a better view to feast on. Matthew was gripping tightly to his handle bars, "But, Dad, I want you to meet my new friend!"

Again, just as sternly as before, "I said get your butt in the house!"

Bruce looked and pointed to Marcus, "And you get out of here!"

Matthew was starting to cry. "But, Dad, that is Marcus, my new friend!"

Again, but yelling this time, "Get in the house now!"

Matthew dropped his bike and started sobbing and ran into the house. Marcus was already crying and running down the sidewalk toward his own house, "And don't you ever come back here!"

Phyllis had her nose pressed against the window screen while still holding her curtain back and then stretched her neck as far as she could to see which direction the black boy was running. She quickly ran to the next window to watch him run till he was completely out of her sights.

Two days later in the morning, Phyllis Jones stomped out of the front door, and the screen door snapped back at her husband Carl Jones, as he followed her out with a huge box full of craft supplies. Phyllis was oblivious that Carl was right behind her. She marched out to the mailbox to gather the freshly delivered mail, and while she was flipping through the mail, she yelled, "Carl?" She looked at her watch, "Carl!"

He was standing in the driveway about ten feet from her, but he didn't answer as quickly as she liked. In an exhausted submissive tone, he said, "Honey, I am right here!"

Stern and demanding, she said, "Well, when I call for you, you need to answer right away, so I know that you hear me!" She stepped closer to him with a look of disapproval, straightened his hat on his head, looked down into the box he was holding, and then slowly ran her fleshy sights up till she locked eyes with him. "Is everything that was on my list in here?"

"Yes, I…I believe so."

"Well, where is it?" she barked.

"What are you talking about Phyllis?" Carl answered.

"The list! Where is the list?" Carl sighed heavily, set the box down on the trunk of the car, and pulled the list out of his shirt pocket. Phyllis quickly snatched the list from Carl's hand and examined the contents of the box. "Where are the pipe cleaners? There are no pipe cleaners!" Carl stepped closer to Phyllis to look at the list she was now holding. "There are no pipe cleaners on your list!" Carl stated.

At that moment, Bruce Thomas from across the street came out of his front door, and the screen door slammed shut behind him. As Bruce walked toward the mailbox, he tripped over a jump rope, and it got caught on his ankle. He did a few hops and kicks before it let go of him, "What the heck! Girls, get this picked up!"

Phyllis was watching Bruce over the top of her list. She gave a disapproving look of disgust and a roll of her eyes as she adjusted her cat eyed glasses and did a "tsk" of her tongue. From a tree closest to the road on Bruce's property, Millie (Matthew's older middle sister) was sitting in the tree, humming softly, "Santa Claus Is Coming To Town," and blowing bubbles. Several bubbles escaped the tree and floated over to where Carl and Phyllis were standing. Phyllis, with an irritated look, started swatting them away and as she looked over to the Thomas's house to see where they were coming from, a huge soapy bubble splatted (pop!) on her left lens of her perfectly clean specks!

Phyllis flinched in a big way. She took off her tainted glasses and started to hysterically grumble her normal snobbery, "Oh my word! Kids these days! They have no sense! I am just so fed up with—" Phyllis instantly stopped her ranting when she looked up from cleaning her glasses with Carl's shirt tail and saw Millie climbing out of the tree. In a massively fake higher voice, she said, "Oh! Well, hello there, Molly!"

Millie was laughing silently to herself. Sarcastically, and with one hand on her hip, she said, "It's Millie! Hi, Mrs. Jones!"

"Are all you children going to church camp tomorrow?" Phyllis poured as much sugar on her words as possible. Millie answered politely just to amuse her, "We sure are. Yes sir-re!"

Phyllis returned, "That's good. We're going to have fun, fun, fun!"

Millie was already heading for her house, and under her breath, she said, "Ugh, what a witch!" She continued humming "Santa Claus Is Coming to Town.'"

Next morning

It was a beautiful summer morning, not a cloud in the sky, and the forecast for the ten days of camp was looking hopeful. Millie Thomas was already out front of her house jumping and skipping her rope on the sidewalk when she saw Phyllis and Daniel leave for church camp. Millie knew they always went extra early to make sure everything was set up and to help greet and get all the kids to their assigned cabins.

The younger "Day Camp" kids had their own special gathering spot too. It was a tradition around these parts, and most of the regulars were spending the school year sharing memories and inviting the new kids in town to the next year's Heartland Church Camp. Every age group had special things to do. Of course Bible lessons and church in the tabernacle, along with craft making, a nice play ground, kick ball, volleyball, baseball, basketball, swimming, choir, and music competitions. There were sing-a-longs around the camp-fires in the evenings, and they always had some of the best cooks from the area churches that volunteered to fix the food and baked goods for the cafeteria. If you were going into kindergarten to twelfth grade, Heartland Church Camp was the place to be. Area churches would sponsor many children for the families that couldn't afford to send their own. No one wanted a child to miss out on this special experience.

Matthew was up stairs in his room trying to decide what else to pack for camp besides his guitar. He saw his marble bag sitting open on his nightstand, and as he tried to close it by pulling the drawstrings, a couple of marbles rolled out. With a quick reflex, he tried to catch them before they got away. He accidently knocked over his plastic glass of grape juice, which was half full and was also on his nightstand. It landed on his throw rug that was lying by his bed and it left a huge stain. Fearfully, he put his hands on his face and whispered, "Oh no!"

Betty (Matthew's oldest sister) was coming down the stairs, and as always, chomping on bubble gum, carrying her bag in one arm, and her diary and favorite book in the other hand. In the kitchen, there was plenty of evidence of a violent event last night. A few bruises on Maxine Thomas gave confirmation that she was there. She was trying to pick up, along with trying to get the children corralled to get their stuff into the car, then get them dropped off at church camp in time. Choking back emotions, Maxine cleared her throat and yelled, "You kids ready to go?" Millie gave an urgent response from the sidewalk, "Coming, Mom!" Millie quickly dropped her jump rope and ran inside to get her things. She headed in the front door, and as Matthew was coming out with his stuff, he announced loudly, "Shotgun! My turn to sit up front!" Matthew tossed the rest of his belongings in the trunk of the Oldsmobile, and Millie came flying back out of the front door with hers. Maxine followed, carrying her purse and wearing a lightweight sweater, which it was clearly too warm to be wearing that for sure, but the children didn't whisper one word to question if she were too warm. They knew, they all knew.

Matthew sat shotgun, Betty sat behind her mother, and just as Millie crawled in the seat behind Matthew, she said, "Wait! I forgot something!" She hopped out and ran over to the sidewalk to retrieve her jump rope and hurried back to the car.

You could hear a train whistle blow as they were drawing nearer to the railroad tracks and the rail-crossing bar began to lower. Maxine's car was first in line at the tracks in front of the stop arm, and they all looked over at the depot where the passengers had already boarded the train and it was ready to leave the station. Matthew looked over at the nearest house across the tracks and saw Marcus and his mother loading the trunk of the car with what looked like camping gear. Matthew had a twinkle in his eye with the hope that Marcus was going to Heartland Church Camp too, even though they didn't have time to talk about it yet.

Meanwhile, the train switch operator came out, put a special key in a slot, and pulled a lever to switch the track so the passenger train could leave the station on time. Maxine was trying to be invisible until the train went by, so she looked out the driver side window and did a double take glance at the local gun store. She checked her sunglasses and her bangs in the exterior side mirror to make sure they were covering her bruised eye and forehead as she started to fantasize.

She saw herself holding a gun and pointing it at Bruce…bang!

Just at that moment Maxine sat up straight and looked in the rearview mirror and saw Betty's face full of gum that had just exploded loudly. Maxine started to sweat. She slid her sunglasses back in place and took one more look in the mirror to assure they were covering everything.

After crossing the tracks and leaving town, Matthew started messing with the sun visor while squinting and complaining about the sun being in his eyes. Nothing was helping because he was too short. "I can't get the sun out of my eyes!" Maxine took another look in the mirror at her disguise, and without one hesitation, she grabbed Bruce's reflective sunglasses off the dash and handed them to Matthew. All three children froze at the thought of what she was allowing. With passive aggressive assurance, she said, "Here, you can use these! Just make sure you give them back when we get to camp." Matthew carefully took them without touching the lenses and put them on and looked in the mirror. He ran his fingers through his hair and was feeling more grown up with each passing second. Matthew sat back in his seat with great posture and a rare confidence. A super hero smile formed on his face as he looked out his side window.

As they arrived at camp, Maxine found the furthest parking spot away from all the other cars in the lot, and it just happened to be by a big bush. It seemed like a safe nonconspicuous place and afforded an easy quick exit. Matthew, Millie, and Betty got out and met their mom, unlocking the trunk; and Maxine hugged and kissed each one of her children before they gathered their belongings. Their friends were waving to the Thomas kids as they were walking away from the car with their camping gear.

Many children that had already arrived were playing on the grounds, and several girls were jumping rope over by the swings. Like a periscope, Phyllis Jones was observing the arriving campers, supervising with her clipboard in hand, but then she spotted Maxine. Out of the corner of Maxine's eye, she saw that Phyllis recognized her, and she started moving in her direction waving her arm, "Oh hi, Maxine! I just have one question for you! Will you…ahhh…"

Maxine was not in the mood to get stuck being interrogated by her nosy neighbor about some loud noises she may have heard last night. Maxine gave a forced smile and a small wave of recognition and turned away quickly as if she couldn't hear anything she was saying. Maxine was very aware that other cars were arriving and parking way too close for her comfort, so she closed the trunk and went for the driver's door. Just before she opened the car door, she noticed a beautiful fuzzy bee on the side mirror. She stopped, and they shared a freeze frame moment of a peculiar, yet sweet connection. She opened the door, and when she closed it, the bee flew away.

Maxine was frantically fumbling around, trying to find the right key to start the car and she dropped them on the floor. Fearfully she whispered, "Oh no!" Maxine bent down feeling everywhere trying to search for them.

Matthew walked toward Marcus and gave half a smile and a small wave of his hand. Marcus did the same. A new girl named Sally came strolling up to Matthew, and she noticed her own reflection in his glasses and said, "Wow! Cool glasses! I've never seen that kind before!"

Matthew's mouth dropped open, "Oh no!"

Of course, Daniel was watching, always lurking for another opportunity, and approached. "Those aren't his, those are his dad's glasses aren't they, Matthew?"

Sally replied, "I don't care. They look cool on you!" She was obviously amused with Matthew and could have cared less about Daniel's presence.

Daniel was really trying to turn on the charm and lure her way from Matthew. So, he stepped in closer and looked directly at Sally and said, "This is your first time here at camp, right? If you were here before, I am sure I would have remembered you."

Sally was ignoring Daniel all together and didn't even acknowledge that he said anything to her, but Matthew had her full attention.

Maxine finally found her keys, but she was having trouble getting her car started, and she was in a panic to leave before Phyllis got to her to interrogate and question her with Phyllis' good godly advice. Most of all, she didn't want her to see her bruised and swollen face.

The car still wouldn't start, "Come on, come on, come on. Oh, please start!"

Meanwhile, Phyllis looked over at her son Daniel and spun on the ball of her foot and instantly changed her direction. Maxine just fell off her radar, and she was in hot pursuit of another target. Marching right back to where she came from, Phyllis put her hand on her hip while still holding her clip board and said sharply, "Hey, little missy, I think you better get back over there with the other girls instead of over here flaunting yourself in front of the boys!" Sally was embarrassed and ashamed by what Phyllis just said in front of everyone. "But I was just telling him how much I liked his sunglasses," Sally said softly. "I don't care what you were saying. It isn't right for you to be over here hanging out with the boys," Phyllis snapped as she pointed her witchy finger to the direction she wanted Sally to exit. Sally dropped her head with a look on her face like what just happened? She walked away with tears welling up in her eyes.

The bee returned to Maxine's car door mirror, and they locked eyes once again, and at that moment, the car engine revved up and started. The bee flew away. Maxine gave a huge sigh of relief, shifted the car into reverse, and looked out of the rear view window to back the car out of the parking spot.

Matthew turned pail, he stood frozen in tremendous fear. Marcus stepped in a little closer and said, "Are you okay?" Matthew carefully took off his dad's glasses and looked back to where they had parked the car to see if his mom was still there. All he saw was the back end of the car leaving Heartland Church Camp. Matthew hung his head, dropped his shoulders, looked at the dirt, and said, "I'm dead!" Daniel watched intently as this moment unfolded. With a devilish look on his face, he was already calculating how to make more trouble for Matthew. The church bell started ringing in the background.

CHAPTER 2

Forty Years Later...System on Test

Forty years later...

It was an early August morning and fifteen-year-old Danny Junior was riding his bike in the middle of the street delivering newspapers to those people who still enjoyed the news on paper, rather than reading it on the Internet. Danny Junior just kicked over the trash can of one of his customers, then threw the newspaper into the yard, and sped off down the road. The rolled up paper just happened to land in a large fresh pile of dog poop.

A bee buzzed by the muddied morning news in print, then landed on the windowsill of that resident. The bee was looking at a man, still sleeping in his boxers with the sheet just covering his rear enough to expose a scar on his lower back. The room seemed to lack a women's touch, and the walls were barren of expression, but in the corner was a dusty guitar case with random what nots piled on top. It was more of a piece of furniture than a tool that could express vibrations of the heart. The alarm clock stopped the observation, and the bee outside the window flew away.

Matthew turned his alarm off and headed for the bathroom to shower. Meanwhile, the preset coffee pot in the kitchen started to brew. In no time, the coffee started to flow over the outside of the pot onto the counter top, down the cupboards, and then onto the floor.

Matthew was almost dressed, and while buttoning up his work shirt, he looked out the window and noticed someone had tipped over his garbage can again! "S———t!" he said under his breath. He headed to the kitchen to retrieve his coffee and saw the mess, and a little louder now, "S——t!" Quickly, he put the pot correctly in its place to see if he could at least get a partial cup-of-joe for the road. He grabbed a few rags from the laundry room and started cleaning up the mess.

Matthew then headed out the front door to retrieve the morning paper and saw the headlines were completely smeared with a massive pile of dog poop. "S——t!" He carefully picked up the soiled newspaper and walked it over to his dumped trashcan, set it upright with his free hand, and then tossed it in. Several beer cans and empty liquor bottles and other trash had to be picked up too. Matthew looked over at his work van, with ABO Securities written on the sides, and shot a look at his watch. He got in his work van, and before he put his sunglasses on, he checked his gas gauge, and it was almost on empty, "Ugh!" He started the engine then headed for the nearest gas station.

As he approached, he saw the "enter" sign, turned in, pulled up to the pump, and started filling it up. Matthew headed for the station door and looked at the "enter" sign on the door and walked in. While pouring a large cup of coffee, Matthew spotted his paperboy in the station store. Calmly Matthew said, "Hey, Danny, did you knock over my garbage can again?"

With a devilish look in his eye, Danny said, "No! I wouldn't do that!" as he slipped an unpaid candy bar into his side pocket of his shorts. Matthew saw him shoplift it but held his tongue while Danny quickly went out the door, hopped on his bike, and rode away. Matthew picked up a fresh newspaper, laid it on the counter with his coffee, left enough money to cover the missing candy bar, and said, "Keep the change!"

A bee was sitting on the driver's side exterior mirror of his work van and watched Matthew as he walked past the station window, holding his coffee and newspaper under his arm, but the reflection in the window was of the younger Matthew, dressed the same as he was at church camp, but he was mirroring the actions of Matthew as an adult, carrying a comic book and soda.

Matthew neared the enter sign of ABO Securities, stopped at the door, slid his access card to enter the company door, and walked in. "Good morning!" from a cheery coworker.

"Morning," Matthew grunted as he wasn't in the mood to engage with anyone on this lousy morning so far.

In walked a braggadocios fellow employee speaking loudly and arrogantly, "Hey, did anyone read the newspaper this morning? My son, Danny Junior, was picked for the little league 'all-star' tournament!" Daniel Jones continued on while nudging and poking coworkers, trying to get them to engage him as they were standing around waiting for their work orders. They were all trying to get away as soon as possible, and no one wanted to hear Daniel blather on again about his self-righteous, monster of a son!

Matthew hurried out of the disappearing crowd of technicians to pick up parts before leaving for his scheduled route for the day.

Matthew arrived at another enter sign of the first inspection on his route and pulled up to the guard shack to check in with the security guard. Just after Matthew signed in, his work phone rang. "Hello, this is Matthew!"

"Hey, Matthew, this is Joe!" It's Matthew's supervisor. "Daniel Jones needs your help on a residential ASAP. I need you to clear what you are doing and head over to this address that I'll text you, and go help him out"

"Got it. I am on my way!" Matthew said.

"Thanks, bud, I appreciate it!" Joe hung up.

Matthew hung up and threw his phone on the seat, "S———t!"

Matthew looked at the guard with the clipboard, "Well, scratch that, Fred, I'll be back tomorrow instead. Thanks!" He shook his head, rolled his eyes and shifted his van into drive to turn around.

Matthew pulled up to the address that his boss had text him and saw that Daniel's work van was already there. Matthew walked around to the back of his van to retrieve his tool belt and put it on. He started walking across the street to the house and a siren was heard. Around the corner came a fire truck with its flashing lights, and it stopped right in front of the house that he was sent to work on.

The fire chief hopped out of the truck looking angry, in fact very ticked off, while looking at both ABO vans sitting on the street, and then he focused on Matthew's ID badge. The fire chief, spouting with attitude, said, "You know you got a fire alarm at this house going off?"

Matthew, lifting one arm in the air with his palm up, said, "Hey, I just got here. I know this house has issues with their alarm, that's why we are here today!"

Fire chief picked up his radio and spouted, "Unit 24 to dispatch!"

Inside the house, Daniel was smirking while peeking through the blinds, watching Matthew get grief from the fire chief. Daniel could hear the heated voice of the fire chief as he went on and on about the false alarm—that they should be fining ABO Securities for running their butts over here, when they should only be called out for someone in real need.

As the fire truck was leaving, Matthew headed to the front door, and Daniel opened it slowly before he knocked. "Hey, ya made it!" Daniel said with a look that Matthew wanted to just smack off his face.

"What the hell, Daniel! Didn't you call in and put this house on test?" Matthew said with his teeth clinched.

Daniel, acting all innocent, said, "Hey, I just came from the other room, what's up?"

"You sent out an alarm from this place, and the fire chief is up in my face about, getting falsely called out here again and wants to fine ABO Securities for your screw up!"

Daniel said, "Who cares. I ain't payin' for it!"

Matthew shot back, "Yeah, dude, that's all you care about—yourself!"

Matthew stepped in through the doorway past Daniel, he could hardly believe the smell and the mess that these people lived in. Matthew whispered under his breathe, "Are you kidding me?" as he continued to look across the entire living room from wall to wall. "I think I am going to be sick!" Daniel waved one hand around and said, "Hey, after a while you get used to the smell! Let's start trouble shooting."

Matthew said, "How about right after you call and put this system on test!"

Daniel started laughing. "Oh yeah, my bad!"

They split up, each going in different directions. Daniel headed down what was left of a hallway, there was so much stuff everywhere that there was only a small path in between all the pack ratted crap. Matthew stepped into what he thought to be the kitchen. He scanned the room and finally saw what had to be the top of the refrigerator and also located the sink faucet amongst the dishes and boxed food and cans that were probably expired. It looked like an avalanche was about to happen on the countertop.

He located the smoke alarm with a flashing red light, which was why the false alarm had been calling the fire department out. Matthew had to move stuff off of the chair so he could use it to reach it. He finally got the cover off the detector loose, and as soon as he removed it, a few cockroaches fell out onto him. "Ahh." Matthew jumped off the chair rubbing his hands all over him. "They don't pay me enough for this s———t!" Trying to gather himself with the assurance that they weren't still on him, he got back up on the chair and cleaned out the debris and waste from the bugs.

His next stop was the attic. Matthew was pouring with sweat as he was bent over working, and his shirt was hiked up just enough to expose the scar on his lower back. Of course, Daniel showed up when he was just about finished, "Hey, what happened to your back? What's the scar from?"

Matthew's cell phone rang with a funny ring tone, and Daniel loudly resounded, "Pffft! Hahaha!" Matthew shot Daniel a look that could kill and took his phone out of his clip on his belt to check the caller ID. He sharply pushed ignore and placed his phone back in his belt.

Daniel continued, "So, how did you get that scar on your back man?"

"It's not important right now! It's hot as hell up here, and I just want to get out of this hoarder's mess!" Matthew snapped back. He wiped his face with a sweat towel that he kept in his tool belt, then his cell phone made a sound that let him know he had a voice mail. He closed his eyes and slightly shook his head.

Matthew arrived home after work, threw his keys on the table, then pulled his phone out, and noticed the reminding icon that he had a voice mail waiting, but he laid down his phone and added to the pile of keys. He walked over to the cupboard, grabbed a glass and poured himself a stiff drink, took a long drink, and swallowed hard; and his faced told that it burnt. Matthew picked up his cell phone once again and pushed the voice mail button…

"Hi, Matthew, this is Aunt Florence. Just wanted to remind you of the family reunion coming up this Labor Day. We sure hope you can come this year, not the same without you! Same place, same time!"

Matthew closed his eyes, dropped his head, and said, "S——t!" and finished his drink.

The next morning at 6:00 a.m., Matthew pulled up to Hector's Café. He looked at the "Enter" sign on the door as he opened it. A bell with a rusty patina hanging on the door announced that someone else had arrived. Matthew walked over to the bar, plopped down on a stool, and grabbed a menu.

Hector the owner and the best-known cook in town, was cooking hash browns, bacon, and eggs, and flipping pancakes on the grill. He bent down to look through the pass thru to see how many just walked through the door at the tone of the bell. "Mornin', Matthew, what brings you in so early?" said Hector.

The waitress walked toward him with a fresh pot of coffee. Matthew turned his cup over with a gesture to fill it up. He looked up and replied to Hector and said, "Bank inspection, I have to get it done before they open."

A man a couple stools from him made an announcement to all that was sitting at the breakfast bar about the all-star little league game coming up. Matthew didn't respond as he kept his nose in the menu but raised one eyebrow at just nearly hearing that kid's name sent a wave of annoyance through his soul! With his face still planted in the menu, he told the waitress, "I'll take the Hector's special with double bacon, hash browns nice and crispy, eggs over easy, no slime, blueberry pancakes, and lots of coffee!"

The waitress said, "Got it!" She leaned in with a wink and a nod, "Now you best get started on that coffee! I'll be back with your order in a few."

Matthew finished his breakfast and walked across the street to get his tools and badge out of his van, then headed for the front door of B. Haven Bank. He took one of his keys and tapped it on the glass door to get the security guards attention. The guard waved as Matthew held up his badge. Then the guard unlocked the door and let him in. Matthew said kindly to the guard, "Will you please let your manager know that I am here for the scheduled inspection of the bank's alarm system."

Security guard said, "Sure thing, Matthew!"

While Matthew was waiting in the lobby, the maintenance guy gestured from the ladder while changing blown light bulbs on the chandelier, "Hey, could you please hand me that pack of light bulbs?"

Matthew answered, "Sure thing! Wow, you've got a lot burnt out there."

Maintenance guy replies, "Yeah, I know, it'll keep me busy for a while!"

The bank manager walked up and greeted him with a firm handshake and smile. "Hey, Matthew, glad to see it is you this time!"

"Hi, Dean, I'm here to do your inspection."

Matthew smiled back. Dean pointed to the counter, "You know the routine. I need you to sign in." As Matthew finished his signature, he said, "I need to sign into the keypad, check the main control, and we can get the escorted witnessed parts done first, the vault and ATMs before you open for business."

Dean shook his head in agreement, "Sure thing Matthew!"

A few hours, later that same morning, at a local drugstore that was just up the street from the B. Haven Bank, the doorbell got the attention of a young male teenager clerk who had been stocking shelves. As the clerk caught a glimpse of who it was, he ducked out of sight into a section behind the cashier who was checking out the purchases of an elderly women. The teenage clerk watched the surveillance monitor and pressed record on the location of Danny Junior.

Danny Junior walked around the store all cocky and full of himself, looked at random stuff, and purposely knocked things over and made no attempt to pick any of it up. Danny Junior stopped at the magazines, picked several up, and while flipping through them, scanned his eyes around to see if anyone was watching him. The teenage clerk was still watching Danny Junior on the TV monitor, but Danny Junior was clueless that he was being watched.

He spun the sunglass display around, and while he had tried several pairs on, he still thought he was clever as he looked around to see if anyone was paying attention to him. In a quick smooth move, he slid a pair of dark non-reflective sunglasses into the side pocket of his shorts and headed for the door. As he walked through the door, the alarm went off. Danny Junior ran toward his bike. The teenaged clerk boldly shouted and was ready to pursue, "Hey! I'm gonna get his ass!" The clerk ran out the door!

Matthew just exited the bank and heard yelling up the street so he looked up. The store clerk was running out of the drugstore in hot pursuit of Danny Junior peddling hard on his bike. Danny Junior pulled out the sunglasses from his leg pocket on his shorts and had the nerve to put them on. As he looked back over his shoulder with a proud smirk on his face, he started peddling faster when he noticed the clerk was not far behind him. Danny Junior took one more look to see where the clerk was, and he peddled himself right into the "enter" sign of the drive thru.

Matthew watched as Danny Junior hit the sign and rolled off his still moving bike. The teenage clerk yelled while approaching, "You punk thief, you deserve that!" The clerk came to a stop, bent over, and held his knees, trying to catch his breath, and not giving a care if Danny Junior might be hurt or not. The clerk took out his phone and took a picture.

Matthew ran across the street to see if Danny Junior was okay. The clerk was still rambling on, "He finally got what he deserved!"

Matthew said, "What's going on?" while bending down to check on Danny Junior.

"Caught him stealing those sunglasses, and I got him on the store video and everything," the clerk said while still breathing heavily. "Last week this little sucker keyed my car and slashed my tire!" Danny started to moan.

Matthew said to the teenage store clerk, "You better call 911!"

"Hell no, he can die for all I care," spouted the clerk. Matthew pulled out his phone and dialed 911.

Matthew and the clerk were still talking to the police officer as they were loading Danny Junior into the ambulance. Matthew got back into his van with very mixed emotions as he watched the ambulance pull away in his rear view mirror. Starring into space momentarily, he finally picked up his work phone and started dialing. "Joe, this is Matthew. I am running behind this morning. I finished the B. Haven Bank inspection, and as I was coming out, I witnessed a bad accident." He paused. "It was Daniel's son."

Later that evening, Matthew was sitting at a local sports bar, eating his last chicken wing and taking the last swig of beer. He motioned to the bartender to bring another one. The bartender nodded, "Coming up!"

Another employee of ABO Securities came walking into the bar and saw Matthew sitting by himself watching TV. He saddled up onto the next stool beside him and said, "Hey, Matthew, you mind if I join you?"

"Sure, Sam, go right ahead." Matthew greeted as he slid him the bucket of peanuts and caught the eye of the bartender and said, "Make that two!"

"Thanks man," said Sam. "Did you hear about Daniel's son?"

Matthew took a long drink and set down his second beer, "Yeah, I saw the whole thing happen." Sam leaned in, "No kidding? What happened?"

"He was riding his bike pretty fast because the drugstore clerk was chasing him on foot. Danny turned around to see where he was at, and he rode his bike right into the Enter sign of the Drive Thru."

Snickering, Sam said, "Seems like a grand slam to me!"

They both laughed out loud. "Sorry, but that little prick had it coming!" Matthew said as he cracked another peanut.

"I'd say! Wonder how Daniel's gonna brag about this one?" replied Sam.

Both chuckled again and nodded in agreement. Matthew said, still chewing, "I don't know, but I had to call 911 because the store clerk wouldn't do it."

Sam replied sarcastically, "Daniel will be charred because there wasn't a parade on the way to the hospital." Both started laughing and clicked their bottles together.

Matthew almost choked, "Good one! Well at least he did get some flashing lights out of it!"

"So why was a store clerk chasing him?" Sam wondered.

"The clerk was a teenager and he said he caught Danny Junior on video stealing sunglasses. He had them on his face when he crashed. The tag was even still on them," Matthew reported.

Sam responded, "Wow! Think Daniel will believe it? Or do you think Daniel will make Danny Junior out to be the victim?"

Matthew rolled his eyes. "Who knows? The clerk even said he keyed his car and slashed one of his tires after the game the other night."

Sam paused. "It will be interesting to see how Daniel swallows this. The rotten apple doesn't fall far from the ol family tree!"

Two days later in the morning

Several employees were standing around while others were sitting at the long table in the conference room. Joe, their supervisor, walked in closing the door behind him and laid a pile of papers on the table. Joe cleared his throat. "Ah, many of you might have heard that Daniel Jones's son, Danny Junior, was in a bicycle accident a day and a half ago. I just got word early last evening that Danny Junior didn't make it." Matthew's eyes got big, and at the same time. Sam and Matthew looked at each other with shock on their faces.

"He made a sudden change for the worst, and must have had some internal bleeding that they were not aware of. He passed away late afternoon yesterday." Joe announced.

You could have heard a pin drop in the conference room. "So...," Joe continued, "I have made a few changes in everyone's schedules for the next week, and I will allow a couple of hours excused for those of you who wish to attend Daniel's son's funeral, which I hope many of you do go. I will be attending also, but no one gets excused time off if you don't go. It will otherwise cost you points if you want to play hooky."

Joe started passing out the schedules with the employees' names on them. "Also enclosed is the info on the time and place of Danny Junior's funeral and your individual changes to your current schedules due to Daniel being off for bereavement. I have evenly divided up Daniel's schedule between all of you, and I want to thank you in advance for everyone's cooperation in this matter."

A few days later, Matthew and Sam were standing about eight feet outside of the grave sight tent while the preacher was reading a passage from the Bible. Everyone had their heads bowed, but Matthew looked up because he heard buzzing. He looked over to his slight right, and there was a huge fuzzy bee, hovering in one spot looking right at him. They stared at each other and were sharing a strange but divine connection at that moment, then the bee buzzed away.

It was strange because it was as if no one heard the buzzing, which seemed very loud to Matthew. The preacher continued quoting scripture. Phyllis Jones looked at Carl Jones's headstone that was next to where Danny Junior was being buried. She started an obnoxious and overly done performance of high pitched crying and carrying on while holding her hand to her chest. She dabbed her eyes with her foo-foo lacy hanky while peeking over the top of her cat eyes glasses to see if anyone was observing her show. After watching Phyllis' stage play, Matthew rolled his eyes and bowed his head.

Matthew heard the loud buzzing. The bee returned and did the same thing again! Matthew was somewhat amused and looked over at Sam to see if he was aware of what was happening. Sam looked at Matthew and moved his eyebrows to let him know that he saw it too. The bee was still hovering and looking at Matthew. After a long moment, the bee flew off again, but he watched it fly over the tent and disappear as the graveside service was ending.

As friends and family were returning to their cars, Matthew stopped at another gravestone—"Bruce Thomas 1925–1985." He hesitated for a brief moment while staring at the head stone, then suddenly moved away and headed straight to his car.

That evening

Matthew was sitting in his favorite chair in his living room as the light was giving way to dusk. He poured more alcohol into his almost empty glass and starred at the pile of newspapers that Danny Junior had delivered over the past few weeks. He drank what he just had poured into his glass, closed his eyes, and waited for the booze to bring him to the chemical induced zone of relief for his mourning.

CHAPTER 3

Test Signal Brings Glimmers of Hope

Midafternoon, the Friday before Labor Day

Matthew opened the door to his work van, hopped in, and laid his tool belt on the floor. He was just finishing up some paperwork before heading to his next stop. He picked up the schedule to look up the next address left on his route for the week. "What the hell? No way!" he yelled as he threw his head back hard onto his headrest. After a brief moment, he picked up his phone and dialed his supervisor. "Joe, this is Matthew. Hey, I am not going to have time to make it to 301 Lane Avenue."

Joe cut him off, "Sorry, Matthew, you are just going to have to make time for it even if it means overtime. Daniel is still out on bereavement, and everyone else is loaded up too. We just can't afford getting behind on scheduled appointments. So suck it up and just get it done. Besides, you are one of our best technicians."

Matthew was staring into the rearview mirror, and he numbly said, "Okay, later!" He hung up the phone and tossed the phone on the seat next to him. He began hitting his hands on the steering wheel, then grabbed it tightly with both hands, "S——t...s——t!"

He was approaching the unwanted address on his work order. "If I just would have looked at my schedule earlier, I could have traded with someone, but no, it's too late now!" he babbled to himself. With his window down and his arm resting there, he pulled across the street from the house to park and turned the engine off. He sat there for a long moment and held his breath as he slowly looked at the house and it looked just like it did in 1966.

The jump rope was on the sidewalk. The man wearing black boots, jeans, white t-shirt with cigarettes rolled up into the sleeve, was under the hood of the car. Two young boys were standing there— Marcus and himself. Bruce yelling, "And you get out of here!"

"But, Dad, that is Marcus, my new friend!"

"Get in the house. Now!"

He was sweating now and he took off his sunglasses to wipe his face with his hand. Still stalling, he reached over and slammed a huge drink of water. He grabbed his tool belt and paperwork and started the dreaded walk toward the front door. Matthew rang the door-bell. Then again. Finally, the door opened. "Hello! Can I help you?" Matthew cleared his throat. "Yes! Mr. Williams? I am Matthew from ABO Securities, and I am here about the alarm system." He showed him his ID badge.

"Oh yes. Come on in," Mr. Williams said as he opened the door wide and stepped aside. Matthew entered. "Sorry about the mess, but I bought this place about six months ago."

Matthew caught himself looking at the stair steps where a chip of wood was missing. Mr. Williams kept talking while Matthew was having another flashback.

Bruce came through the front door and threw a wrench into the stairs, which caused the missing chip of wood in the second step, then shoved something in the hall wastebasket on the way to the kitchen for a beer.

Matthew pulled his focus away from the staircase and took a step back as he lifted his paperwork up to his face to help snap him-self back to reality. "And started to do some remodeling, and I just moved in about two weeks ago and wanted the alarm system put back into service," Mr. Williams finished.

Matthew gathered himself, "Looking at the paperwork, and if I understand you correctly, you want the alarm system put back in service and a smoke detector added upstairs. Is that correct?"

Mr. Williams nodded, "Yes, that's correct, but I am also con-cerned about my office window being protected too because of the lattice that is right outside the window, someone could climb up it. I would rather protect the window than take down the lattice. I like it!"

"Okay," Matthew said as he marked his paperwork. "From what I see of the system that was active before, all the windows were protected on the first floor, but I will be testing the entire system after I add on the extras you want. Is that okay?"

Mr. Williams replied, "That would be great!"

Matthew put his clipboard down by his side, trying to be calm, and said, "All I need from you now is the location of the main control, keypad, and the attic access. (Like Matthew didn't already know!)"

Mr. Williams pointed. "The main control is in the basement under the stairs, and that door is the second door on the left, and the key pad is right there."

Matthew's knees were feeling weak as the familiarity of this house was getting under his skin, yet he forged ahead as he followed the new owner upstairs. Mr. Williams opened the door to his office.

Matthew saw himself as a young boy running into the room and diving onto the stained rug and crawling quickly under the bed.

Matthew grabbed the doorjamb to steady himself. Mr. Williams was pointing to the closet where the attic access was, "It's up there. The attic door is up there." By this time, Matthew reentered reality and finally got his first glimpse of the office. The desk looked like it was already being used, nodding and acting like he heard everything. Matthew said, "Thank you very much. I think I've got it from here. If I have any more questions, I'll ask you then, if that's okay?"

The cordless phone on the desk started ringing. Mr. Williams walked over to get a look at the caller ID, and it bought a smile. "Ah yes, I have been waiting for this call. I am going to have to take this." He picked up the phone, "Hi, George, I'll be right with you!" He put his hand over the phone and looked at Matthew, "That's fine, Matthew, I will be in the living room if you need me."

He walked out of the office door. Matthew made it to the basement and was standing in front of the alarm's main control. He was connecting the butt set onto the phone lines, and the butt set speakers were on also, so he could hear the other party. He started dialing numbers and tones were heard as he entered them. He heard ringing on the other end, the other party answered, "ABO Securities data team."

"Hello, this is Matthew, tech 52499, I am putting this system back in service." Voice on the phone, "Do you know what the system number is?" Matthew answered, "L183065, I am going to be sending signals to you. I'll need verification that you are receiving them."

The voice on the phone said, "Got it. Are you at 301 Lane Avenue?

"That's it, I will call you back to confirm signals when I am done." Matthew hung up. He reached into his tool belt to retrieve a pair of needle nosed pliers, and before inserting them into the control, he turned the butt set back on and could hear dial tone on the phone again. He touched some connections inside the main control and could hear the alarm system dialing, a modem type tone answered, and several fast tones, then the phone line clicked and was dead again. He removed the butt set from the phone line.

Matthew walked back into the office upstairs and over to the closet and opened it.

He saw his toys on the shelves and his clothes hanging in the closet with his shoes and winter boots on the floor. He closed his eyes, shook his head in distress, and opened his eyes slowly to see if it helped erase the image. "Ah." It left.

Matthew grabbed the ladder that was already in the office, probably from the resent paint job, and he set it up inside the closet so he could reach the attic door on the ceiling. Before he crawled through the door, he tossed up a roll of wire and placed his drill on the edge of the opening. He spotted the chain to turn on the light. He noticed that the roll of wire traveled further than he expected, and it was laying on the insulation between the rafters.

On his hands and knees, he carefully stretched out to retrieve the wire roll. As he looked down to return to a flat surface, he saw part of an envelope sticking up between the insulation and a rafter. Matthew carefully grabbed the aged discolored envelope and slowly turned it over. It was addressed to Bruce Thomas, 301 Lane Avenue.

Matthew grabbed the envelope from under the stained rug by his nightstand, hurried to his closet door, and climbed the shelves till he could reach the attic door. He pulled the chain to turn on the light, shoved the envelope between the insulation and the rafter, and then pulled the chain again—the memory went black.

Matthew was still on his knees, dripping with sweat, and looking at the never opened envelope. He shoved it down deep into his tool belt and got back to work.

Matthew was back in the basement now connecting the wires inside the main control that go to the smoke detector he just installed. The main control box was in a small storage room under the basement stairs. He heard footsteps approaching. Matthew was frozen in fear and was under the basement stairs when he heard footsteps coming down. He saw his dad's black boots through a large knothole from the underside of one of the step boards.

"How's it going?" Mr. Williams asked. As he came through the storage room, he became concerned. "Are you feeling okay?"

Stuttering, he said, "Ah yeah. Yes, I am fine. It was really hot in your attic today, that's all."

He took a towel out of his tool belt and wiped his brow. "I'm just finishing up the smoke detector connections. Then I'll be testing all the protection and everything else to confirm we're transmitting and receiving.

Late afternoon

Matthew was driving home, stress, and relief were all over him at the same time; and he ran his hand through his hair like he was trying to brush it all off of him. He grabbed his water bottle and drank it till it was gone. Just at that moment, he passed by an abandoned place while driving by. He cranked his neck back to get a better look, and then he tried to get one more glimpse in the rear view mirror. He really didn't have a clue why he reacted to that place, but he sat up straighter, grabbed the steering wheel with both hands, and continued driving.

On his way home, he saw an "Enter" sign to a drive-through, and as he turned in, he took off his work ID badge and put it in the glove box. Matthew pulled his work van in the open door. The attendant said, "Hi! What can I get for you?"

"I'll take a supersized root beer and a large bag of barbecued chips."

The attendant answered, "Coming up!" A moment later, he returned with his order. "Anything else today?"

Matthew said, "I'll take a six-pack…no, make that a twelve-pack of Bud Lite in a brown bag."

"Okay, would you like that cold?"

Matthew nodded, "You bet!"

Attendant returned with his beer in a brown bag, "Anything else?"

Matthew smiled and said, "A months' vacation and a shoe box full of twenties!"

Attendant laughed. "You and me both!"

Matthew handed him cash and a hefty tip. "Mum's the word on the brown paper bag and you can keep the change!"

Attendant looked at how much the tip was and said. "No problem! Come again and hope you have a good weekend!"

Matthew exited the drive thru and mumbled sarcastically, "Yeah right! Ugh!"

Matthew unlocked the door to his home, dropped his keys on the table, and set down the brown bag of beer and chips. Tossed his root beer cup in the trash and missed, "S——t!" Picked it up then crammed it in the basket, then gave it a kick. He poured himself a couple shots of Jack Daniels, tossed half of it down his throat, and dropped himself hard into his favorite chair. Trying to relax, he closed his eyes.

In monochromatic setting:

Matthew and his two sisters (at their current ages) were in front of their childhood home, 301 Lane Avenue. The whole place was overgrown with dark vines, so much so that not much sky could be seen. Betty (the oldest sister) walked over to a shrub and tried to break part of the vine off that was suffocating the bush. It turned into powder and disintegrated in her hand. Slowly, another vine that she was not aware of started wrapping itself around her leg and ankle several times. Meanwhile, Millie (the middle sister) walked onto the porch, looking at the windows that were replaced with cement blocks. Matthew was walking toward the house on the sidewalk, and it turned into quick sand, and he started slowly sinking. Betty tried to come to his aid, but the vine drew itself tightly to her leg and she couldn't get free to help him. Matthew continued to sink down to his shoulders, and Millie threw one end of her jump rope toward Matthew. He tried and tried and made every effort to reach it.

Breathing heavily, he attempted pulling himself awake from this disturbing dream, turning his head side to side and finally woke up. He focused on a few family photos that were on the bookshelf then parked his gaze on the family Bible. He paused for a moment then rebelliously drank the rest of his liquor and slammed the glass hard onto the side table and shot up out of his chair quickly. He stomped down to the hallway closet and pulled out a sleeping bag and threw it on the floor with an attitude. He entered his bedroom, changed out of his work clothes to put on well-worn jeans and T-shirt, flung a hoodie over one shoulder, and shut the lights out. He grabbed his sleeping bag and headed to the kitchen. Matthew opened and slammed many cupboard doors until he found his cooler. He filled it with beer and then dumped all the ice he had into the cooler, grabbed the chips and sleeping bag, and then went straight for his truck.

Matthew headed down a country road stuffing his face with chips. He wiped his hand on his pants and saw several crumbs on his shirt and brushed them off too. He reached over to turn on the radio and his hand went right back into the bag of chips. "One Clear Voice" was playing on the radio. He started to take his hand out of the chip bag to change the radio and a few chips fell on the floor, and the bag started to slip. "S——t!"

He tried to save the rest from falling out, which distracted him from retuning the radio. He started swerving some, sat up straight, grabbed the wheel, centered himself, and refocused on the road. The song seemed to calm him, and his hand went back into the chips. This was playing on the radio:

> But all this confusion just disappears
> When I find a quiet place where I can hear.
> One clear voice calling out for me to listen
> One clear voice whispers words of wisdom
> I close my eyes til I find what I've been missing
> And if I'm very still I will hear one clear voice
> (By Peter Cetera)

Matthew slowed down and shut the radio off, turned into an over grown lane and into what looked to be a parking lot at one time. He parked his truck by a huge over grown bush and got out and took a leak. He opened the cooler in the back of his truck and opened another beer, popped it open, and drank half of it in a couple of swallows. Carrying his beer with him he began walking around the grounds.

The sign in front of the lodge was crooked and hanging by one chain instead of two, it says, "HEARTLAND CAMP." The sign was faded and paint was chipping from years of being in the weather and sun. Matthew dragged his finger over the letters as if he were checking to see if they had a pulse. From there, he walked over toward what used to be the playgrounds and swing set, it was depressing and lifeless, full of decay. He strolled over to the lodge where he could now hear faint echoes of cafeteria chatter and laughing. With every step toward the tabernacle, more echoes of "Praise Ye the Lord" song wars were sung between the boys and girls, like a competition of who could sing it the loudest. It brought a slight smile to his face. Maybe the only smile that he had all day. He walked past what used to be the Day Camper area, and he heard echoes of little ones singing:

> Oh, be careful little mind what you think.
> Oh, be careful little mind what you think
> Cause the Father up above
> Is looking down with love
> Oh, be careful little mind what you think

He made his way to the cabins. He was kicking weeds and broken tree branches to the side so he could get a closer look into the windows. He approached one last cabin and set his beer on the windowsill and cupped his hands around his eyes so he could see more clearly. He stopped and focused on a familiar rusty bunk bed frame.

Matthew and Marcus were alone in the cabin and were frantically looking for a place to hide his dad's glasses from Daniel. "Hurry, help me think of a place to hide these. It isn't safe to hide them in my things because that will be the first place that he will look for them! Think, Marcus, think!"

"I don't know, Matthew!" Marcus whispered loudly.

Marcus was looking all around, and then he looked up, "How about up on the wooden beam? Can you reach it from your bed?"

Matthew shouted softly, "Good idea!" He climbed on the top bunk, "Watch the door to see if anyone is coming!" Matthew had to stand on the headboard because he was too short, and he was struggling. Marcus said frantically, "Hurry, someone is coming!" Matthew jumped down off the bed as the screen door opened, and two boys entered the cabin.

Matthew pushed away from the window as if the memory burnt him physically. He picked up his beer and walked away.

Matthew tossed his empty can in the back of his truck, grabbed another beer and downed the entire thing, belched, then smashed the can, and added it to the pile. He picked up his sleeping bag and cooler and walked down another over grown path to a dilapidated bridge that was over the narrowest part of a brook, which lead to a good sized swimming hole. While staggering, he had another flashback of children, running and laughing while racing across the bridge with their towels and swim toys. It seemed so real to him that he actually tripped as if a couple of children bumped into him physically. Once he was in the middle of the bridge, he stopped to get his bearings. He finished another beer and leaned over and saw his faint reflection of the adult Matthew, and he chucked the can into the water. He found a place not far from the bridge to set up camp and plopped his belongings down near a huge tree.

The sun was setting, dusk had rolled in, and Matthew had a decent campfire going. He was thankful that he was in the middle of nowhere, and no one would see his truck for that matter. He wanted to be alone and was glad he didn't even bring his fishing gear. He threw another empty can off to his side and reached in the cooler for another.

He was staring into the fire, the logs were glowing, popping, and shooting sparks in wild rhythmic display. Matthew began murmuring, lifting his face to the star lit sky. "What do you want?"

Long pause. "Where are you?" Another long pause.

"Hey! I'm sending out a test signal to see if you hear me?"

Matthew took another drink as if it would help the matter. "I'd like to confirm we're transmitting and receiving!" Matthew finished and threw this can aside too. Belch! (Long and drawn out)

Matthew looked toward the sky, "That's just what I thought… nothing!"

Matthew laid down on top of his sleeping bag since it was nice out, and any night chill in the air, the campfire took care of that. Matthew finally took his eyes off of the fire and noticed tiny twinkles of light nearby. "Wow haven't seen any lightening bugs in a long time," he mumbled.

As the flames danced about in mystic display over the glowing coals and embers, the snap, crackle, and popping just may be the therapy that he would have to settle for tonight. He readjusted himself and used his hoodie for a pillow and started watching the smoke and sparks travel toward the tree. A soft breeze blew through, lifting the leaves of the tree exposing a city of lights within. Matthew fell asleep.

Matthew was still laying on his side, and he didn't make a move until a sunbeam touched his face. He moaned, rubbed his eyes, and took part of his hoodie and covered his eyes. After a few moments, he moaned, "Ugh," and sat up with an urgency to unload his bladder. Carefully, he slowly got up and staggered to the huge tree so he could lean against it with one arm to urinate. Steading himself, he unzipped and started relieving his tank, along with a loud long backfire.

He heard giggling (still peeing), he looked around to see where it was coming from. He modestly zipped up, turned around, and knocked his head right into a low hanging branch and fell backward onto the ground. "Ah," still lying flat on his back, Matthew brought his hand to his head to see if he were bleeding or not. He turned his head to one side and slowly opened his eyes due to the pain and brightness of the morning sun. He flinched and took a double take, rubbed his eyes once again, and then refocused.

Three bees were each sitting on their own tiny flower and were looking straight at him.

Bee 1 said, "Bee."

Bee 2 said, "Wise"

Bee 3 said, "Zzzzer!"

Matthew's eyes bulged, and he freaked out, "What the #$&%!"

Bee 1, 2, and 3 said in unison, "Beeeeeeep!" to drown out Matthew's bad word. Matthew sat up quickly and butt walked backward about a yard with the help of his hands. The bees flew away. Matthew put his hand over his heart and said, "Dear God, I hope...I hope I haven't—"

Before he could get the rest of his thought out, an adorable firefly showed up, blinking and flashing her divinely original light source. "You called?" Blink, blink, blink. Matthew closed his eyes and shook his head as if he were hallucinating and dizzy from the fall from all the drinking he did last night. He looked up again—blink, blink, blink, blink, blink. The firefly was still there hovering right in front of him.

"I hope. I hope I haven't lost my mind!" Matthew said softly out loud.

"I am still here!" the firefly said.

Staring right at the bug, Matthew said logically and factually, "Bugs can't talk!"

"Well, it's obvious that you don't know everything!" the firefly stated factually.

There was a long awkward pause that made Matthew somewhat relax and consider that this could be very real.

"So what is it you want?" The firefly broke the silence.

Matthew said, "Say what?"

The firefly put one of her legs on her waist and said, "Hey, you are the one that called me. So, what do you want?"

Matthew was totally lost, confused, disoriented, asleep, or dreaming?

"What is going on? I am not kidding here!" Matthew said.

"Did you not just put your hand on your heart and say, 'Dear God I hope?'" the firefly stated.

Matthew said, "I…I think I did. Maybe?"

"Well, you did! It seems to be abundantly clear you don't have a clue how this works," said the firefly as it flashed it's light in a slow fading on and off fashion as if patience were pulsating through it.

"Well, I guess you are right. Maybe I don't."

Matthew was still sitting on the ground, and it was comprehensible that he wasn't sure that he could stand while trying to adjust to having a conversation with a bug.

The firefly said, "Well, let's start this from a different point of view, what my job is, and what my purpose is for! I collect glimmers!"

Matthew scrunched his face and said, "Glimmers?"

"Why, yes!" the firefly stated. "I saw them around you last night!"

"What are you referring to? The sparks from my campfire?"

"No!" waving her front leg at him, "I collect glimmers, expectations, and wishes. I am Hope!"

"Your name is Hope?" Matthew replied.

"Yes, and that is also what I do!" she said. "I collect glimmers of hope!"

She was blinking in a pulsating tempo.

By the look on Matthew's face, you could tell he was going to try and outsmart her, "So where are my glimmers?"

"In your hope chest silly!" Hope laughed.

Matthew looked around for it and said, "Sorry, I don't see it!"

"Wow, you really are in preschool when it comes to this stuff!" Hope rolled her eyes.

"Your hope chest is not out here. It's in you!

"In me?" Matthew said.

"Yes, you even put your hand on where you are storing it," Hope instructed. "I collect and store your invisible glimmers of hopes, dreams, wishes, and goals until you want to do something with them."

Matthew got side tracked and said, "Like I used to collect fireflies and put them in a jar when I was a kid?"

"No!" she said as she rubbed one of her antennas as if she were grooming it. "You really have this whole thing backward on how this works!" She shook her little head and said, "You don't collect us. We collect for you!"

"So, when I hope something, you gather it?" Matthew said.

"Exactly!" Hope agreed.

Matthew said, "So how do I get what I hope for? Do you get it for me?"

"No!" Hope said. "I am not some fairy or fairy godmother that goes around waving a wand and uses witchcraft to do your selfish biding! That's bad!"

Matthew paused, stared at the ground, and said, "Sorry I am really confused. I am obviously hung over and talking to an insect! No offense."

"None taken!" Hope nodded, "I am very happy in who I am and what I do. Thank you very much!" Hope looked at the scattered pile of cans, "Yes, you did have a lot to drink, but you are about to get sobered up quickly."

Matthew said, "I hope so!"

Hope answered back, "I don't so!"

Matthew replied, "What?

"Matthew, you are saying is wrong!" Hope said. "It's not I hope so. You should be saying, I hope it to be so!"

"If you say, I hope so, there is no glimmer for me to collect or gather," Hope said.

"Hmm?" Matthew replied.

"If you say…I hope it then I can collect or gather the it!" Hope explained.

Matthew was really trying to understand, but he just repeated, "I hope it to be so!"

"There you go! That's better."

She encouragingly replied, "Your test signal was heard, that's why I, Hope, am here."

"Test signal? Heard what?" he said.

"Yes, confirmed!" Hope stated. "Now we are going onto the transmitting and receiving part."

"I need you to trust me, Matthew." Hope blinked steadily.

"You know my name?" he asked.

Hope answered, "Of course I do! Matthew, you have to let go of a few things that you wanted me to keep in your hope chest, that is stored in your heart. I, Hope, can't and don't gather and store those kinds of things for you. You have to get rid of some stuff, or you are not going to have room for what you are about to receive in the transmitting."

Hope said, "Now, faith is the substance of things hoped for, the evidence of things not seen."

Matthew said, "Hey, isn't that in the Bible?"

"Absolutely!" she said, "Are you still with me?"

"Yes, is this a clue hunt?" Matthew sat up a little straighter. "I like this!"

"Back to…I hope it to—" Hope said. "I, Hope, collected the it! Now that's as far as I can take what you hoped for, unless I have your permission for the 'to' part."

"Okay?" Matthew kept listening.

"So the invisible 'it' glimmers have to be taken to someone very, very important," Hope said.

"Who?" Matthew asked.

Hope said, "Are you sure?"

"Yes, yes!" Matthew spoke clearly.

Hope said firmly, "You have to 'enter in,' and once you do, you will never ever be the same again!"

Matthew said, "I don't have much to lose at this point."

Hope warned, "You may be holding on to some stuff that your *will* might not want to let go of."

"Okay! I really do want to know what's next. Will you show me where to take my glimmers to?" Matthew announced.

"Thank you, Matthew, I am pleased to take you to the door!" Hope said as she motioned him to get up off the ground. "I…Hope… it…to," she looked him squarely in the eye, "be so is right in there!"

Matthew was standing up now, "Wait! What door? I don't see a door?"

Hope could see his anxiety and tried to comfort him. "Matthew, do you have a hope chest?"

"Yes!" he said.

Hope continued, "Do you see your glimmers, your glimmers of hopes that are in your hope chest?"

"Yes, I know I have a lot of glimmers in my hope chest," he said.

"Your flesh eyes are not the only eyes you have Matthew!" Hope explained. "You see or know about your hope chest because you see it with your mind's eye."

"Oh! You are right!" Matthew agreed.

Hope said, "It's all about the one and the two trees!"

"The one, two, threes?" Matthew said."

"No! The one and the two trees!" Hope corrected.

Matthew said, "I am lost here."

Hope agreed. "Yes, you are lost, Matthew, but just trust me, you finally made it to the right place!"

"You are talking in riddles, Hope!" he said.

Hope continued, "Did you speak out words as a test signal that you wanted to know if they were being heard?"

Matthew said, "I do that every day at work, Hope."

Hope replied, "I am not talking to you about your flesh job work signals but about the 'word' test signal you put out last night, about if you were being heard or not."

Hope had her front two legs on her waist again.

Ashamed of his behavior and drinking too much, Matthew stated, "I probably said a lot of wrong things last night."

Hope started blinking again. "Matthew, but I saw the huge glimmers in what you spoke last night. I caught them for you!"

"So what are you trying to tell me, Hope?" Matthew questioned.

"I, Hope, caught 'it,' your glimmer in the 'words' you spoke! I can only do my part and I did. The rest is up to you, and I am trying to take you to be so!"

Matthew finally said it out loud, "I'm kinda afraid."

"Matthew, glimmers are light, not darkness," Hope continued. "It is impossible for me to collect darkness. Darkness it just the absence of light, and it has no measurable power over light!" Hope was blinking double time. "Hope is light, Hope is a good thing. I could never lead you into fear or darkness."

"Okay!" Matthew said calmly.

Hope said, "Trust and obey, for there's no other way"

Matthew softly finished her sentence singing, "To be happy in Jesus, but to trust and obey!"

Hope blinked brightly, with her front legs on her heart, "You remembered the one!"

Matthew said, "Wow, we used to sing that here at Heartland Church Camp."

Hope said, "That's because all those 'words' are still here!"

"Hmm?" Matthew looked back at her.

Hope said, "I don't want to get ahead of things, but it will all make sense in time!"

"So, Matthew, are you ready to take your glimmers to be so?" Hope asked.

"Yes, let's go!" he said.

"Sorry, Matthew, you have to do this next part on your own," Hope stated. "I will be right here, but only you can enter in to that tree!"

CHAPTER 4

The tree Encounter... Words of Faith

Matthew looked at Hope and said, "So what do I do?"

Hope said, "The word is nigh thee, even in thy mouth, and in thy heart. That is the word of faith."

Matthew was standing under the huge beautiful tree that he camped by last night. As he gazed upward, the foliage of the tree parted, and the atmosphere encapsulated another dimension behind an unseen force field. The words, "Enter in," were heard and seen as glistening bubbles of purest light that joined themselves together as a parking attendant's gloved hand and were motioning and directing Matthew to come. At that very moment, another glowing clear-bubbled word (about the size of a grape) with a bee inside of the word came down to meet Matthew.

Matthew oddly but freely opened his hand, and the bubble word rested in the palm of his hand. Matthew said, "Are you *be so?*"

The bee answered, "I am a bee and I sow. I am Faith!"

Matthew was truly in awe of the light of life that this Faith bee was in. He lifted his gaze higher into the tree, and it was the most amazing sight he could have ever even dreamed. Small bubbles of light with a single bee in each were floating inside the massive spans of wonderment like a giant snow globe effect. Matthew brought his focus back to the word of Faith that he was still holding.

Matthew heard that familiar buzzing sound again that he heard at the graveside service. At the force field opening, a large bee appeared but was not inside a word bubble.

"Nice to see you again, Matthew!" she greeted. "You can enter in by Faith!"

As he moved his hand, the word, "bubble," floated onto his arm so he could enter in the tree. This word of faith became some kind of access key card to this divine tree. He climbed upon one of the lower branches, but for some reason, he could no longer see the outside of the tree or his campsite. He realized that climbing and entering in seemed effortless.

Somewhat confused, Matthew replied, "You know my name?"

"Hello, my name is Bea Addy Tudes, but you can call me Addy," she said with a proper nod of her head. Calmly and gracefully, Addy said, "Welcome, Matthew, welcome to Words of Faith!"

Addy's spoken words of welcome rose into the air and formed into a flower lei and descended around his neck as if he just arrived at an island of paradise. Matthew became intrigued by what he just saw and heard, which eased him a bit. He just couldn't resist lifting part of the flower lei to take in an aroma that was so heavenly. He breathed in deeply, "Thank you! How do you know who I am?"

Addy lovingly said, "I have known you since you gave your heart to Jesus as a young boy at Heartland Church Camp!"

"Camp…" He paused a moment. "Ugh, I remember this tree, it was here when I went to church camp!" he agreed.

Matthew had a small wave of anxiety run through him as the summer of '66 flashed through his mind. Then he noticed bubbles were coming out of his own mouth as he was speaking. The words were alive as they floated around him, and he started to mildly freak out. He put both hands on his head and closed his eyes, then started to rub his hands all over himself as if they were starting to make him itch.

"What's going on here? These bubbles are coming out of me. Am I dead, have I died and moved on?"

Addy smiled again. "No, Matthew, not yet!"

Matthew said, "Oh, dear God, thank you, but I feel different like way different! I am seeing things, things I have never seen before!"

Addy said reassuringly, "Matthew, you have nothing to be afraid of here, you are safe. You have entered into the words of faith!"

Matthew asked again, "But why am I seeing my words?"

Addy replied, "Let's start at the beginning. Hope sent you here, right?"

"Oh yes, she did!" Matthew said in a logical tone as he looked at the bubbles of light floating and moving everywhere within the tree. "Are these my glimmers?"

Addy answered, "No, those are in your heart."

"Hope said my *be so* is in this tree!" Matthew stated.

"Yes, she is!" Addy nodded. "And you have already met her, but let me introduce you to her properly."

The word of faith was still hovering by Matthew and he focused on Faith. "Matthew, this is Faith, your *be so*!"

Faith did a proper curtsy in the word.

"Hello, Matthew, I am Faith and happy to be your *be so*!"

Matthew opened his palm again, and the word of Faith rested there. "Wow, this is amazing! Hello, Faith, so happy to meet you!"

Faith smiled back at him. Matthew's face was almost enlightened with this introduction to Faith. Matthew said, "I almost feel like a kid again with my new imaginary friend!"

"Well, Matthew, I am not imaginary. I am very real!" Faith pointed out.

Addy spoke up and said, "Entering in to Words of Faith just may be the second best decision you ever made!"

Matthew said, "What was the first best decision?"

Addy returned quickly. "Inviting the Word Jesus into your heart!"

Matthew looked a little ashamed at not knowing the answer to that one. "Oh yeah, Jesus!" Matthew paused a moment and asked, "Why did you call him Word?" Addy and Faith looked at each other, and then Matthew said, "I think Hope was right when she said I was a preschooler when it came to how this all works." Matthew sat up straight and said, "I am all ears!"

Instantly, Matthew became all ears! Ears appeared everywhere on his entire body. He saw himself and said, "What's going on here, is this some kind of joke?"

Addy and Faith started to chuckle. Addy, in a motherly voice, said, "Calm down, Matthew! Use all those ears and listen! Words are seeds! There is no time between seed-time-and harvest in this tree. It happens instantly!"

Matthew spoke with all his ears, "Seed, time, and harvest?"

Addy spoke again, "Words are seeds! See!"

Faith said, "You are what you just said!"

Matthew said, "I need to wake up. I am dreaming. Bees don't talk! People can't see words this is bull crap!"

Instantly, a pile of bull crap landed on the branch. Matthew took his handful of ears, put them up to his mouth covered with ears, and tried to shut himself up from speaking again.

A siren sounded, drumbeats began beating, and buzzing was heard. Worker bees appeared in HAZMAT uniforms, and like a whirlwind tornado, the bees had the mess cleaned up! Matthew sat there, stunned, with all those ears. "Sorry about that!"

Addy and Faith watched Matthew take this information in, and she asked, "Are you ready to just hear instead of being all ears?"

Matthew said, "Yes, but how do I get back to that?"

Addy explained, "Just speak it!"

Matthew carefully chose his words this time. "I would like to hear but not be all ears!"

And just that quickly, Matthew was back to himself. "I better be more careful next time I open my mouth!" Both bees nodded their heads up and down, yes.

Matthew was clearly embarrassed by speaking out stinky mucky words that manifested instantly. With his hand still over his mouth, he lifted his fingers just enough to say, "Sorry!"

Addy addressed him, "Matthew, you have entered in to another dimension, there is no time here! Words are seeds. There is no time between seed, time, and harvest. You say the words and then you have the thing you said. You are speaking things that be not as though they were!"

Matthew carefully let go of his mouth and said with mindful calculation, "So you are saying that if I say corn—" instantly,

Matthew had a cob of corn in his hand, and his eyes grew wide. He swallowed and said, "Wow!"

Addy pointed out, "You might as well eat that, it's been a while since you had anything decent to eat." Matthew said, "I think you are right, thank you!" Matthew started to eat the corn, and with the look on his face, it was more filling than he thought it would be. "That was wonderful!" His countenance changed after he ingested the food.

Addy said, "Matthew, you ate your words! A man shall eat good by the fruit of his mouth."

Matthew slightly nodded his head as he received the revelation of that when he said, "I am really glad I didn't have to eat the pile I spoke out earlier!" Faith, inside the word, giggled.

Addy was smiling too. "Matthew, I am so glad you came back to camp."

Even though Matthew had just eaten and felt better, he looked at her with an emptiness and sadness that came from deep within. "To be honest, Addy, I don't really know what brought me here. I know I gave my heart to Jesus long, long ago. Here I am, in my fifties, and sometimes I feel like a broken kid inside, and I feel so lost and empty. I don't know who I am or what my purpose is for even being here. I don't like my job, I am divorced, lost contact with my kids and I drink too much!"

Matthew was hanging his head, and both eyes were welling up with tears.

Matthew looked up in surprise. "I think that is the first time I ever spoke those words to anybody!"

Addy said, "I am not anybody, Matthew. I have a body, but I am not made of flesh and bone."

Matthew replied, "I think I am beginning to understand that."

Addy smiled. "No pun intended, but you are only at the bee-ginning!"

CHAPTER 5

Faith Comes by Hearing

Addy said, "Matthew, you are more than just your body that tastes, smells, hears, sees, and touches. Your purpose is so much greater than the flesh earth suit, the real you is housed in."

Matthew looked at her with sincerity, "How do I find my purpose, Addy? How do I see deeper or know what to do?"

Addy replied while raising both eye brows, "I want you to really think about what you are asking, and if you are truly ready, willing and able to take the trip?"

Matthew laughed, "Trip? This whole thing is a trip so far."

Addy looked Matthew square into his eyes. "Do you want to really see all of you?"

Matthew stated, "If I am not ready now, then I don't think I ever will be. I am unhappy, alone, and empty. I drink for unknown reasons. I am afraid most of the time, but I don't want to admit it. Here, I sit in a tree full of words of light filled with Faith, sent here by a lightning bug named Hope, and trying to find my *be so*. There is only one thing I can say, *I hope it to be so!*"

Addy smiled. "Well said, Matthew!"

Matthew smiled back at her, and Faith in the word bubble gave a thumbs-up to Matthew while smiling big, and she put her other hand on her heart and patted it!

"Matthew, you asked me earlier why I called Jesus the Word," Addy pointed out.

Matthew nodded in agreement that he really wasn't entirely sure what that meant.

Addy voiced, "In the beginning was the Word, and the Word was with God, and the Word was God. All things were made by him, and without him was not any thing made that was made. In him was life, and the life was the light of men. And the Word was made flesh, and dwelt among us. Word was Jesus's name before he became flesh!"

Matthew's eyes were watching the words that Addy was speaking, and each word bubble coming from her voice produced a Faith (bee) in each one. Matthew opened his mouth in awe of what he just witnessed, "I can hardly believe what I am seeing. I mean I heard every word that you said, but what am I seeing?"

Addy spoke again, "So then faith comes by hearing and hearing by the word of God" (Rom. 10:17).

Of course as she spoke and gave voice to the written Word of God, more Faith-filled words arrived. Addy continued, "The words that I speak unto you, they are spirit, and they are life" (John 6:63). As each Faith-filled word arrived at the sound of her voice, the atmosphere within the tree became energized with power, love, and soundness of peace!

Like a little child, Matthew wanted to try it, "So then faith comes by hearing and hearing by the word of God." (Rom. 10:17) Matthew's voice produced his own faith-filled (bee) words of light that hovered around him personally. It was as if they belonged to just him because the sound of his voice was within each word bubble. Matthew's face was void of loneliness as he witnessed this miracle that he was a part of. "Wow! That just came out of me!" Matthew was stunned.

Addy said, "It surely did!" She had the most humble yet joyful look on her face.

Addy spoke, "In the beginning, God created the heaven and the earth... How? God said, 'Let there be light,' and there was light. God called, God said, God called, God said, God called, and God said. God spoke words filled with faith that brought the unseen into existence with his voice. His words obeyed him. He didn't just think it into being, he voiced it!" (Gen. 1:1, 3).

"Now faith is the substance of things hoped for, the evidence of things not seen. Through faith we understand that the worlds were framed by the word of God, so that things which are seen were not made of things which do appear. But without faith it is impossible to please him: for he that cometh to God must believe that he is, and that he is a rewarder of them that diligently seek him." (Heb. 11:1, 3, 6).

Matthew said, "This is amazing! His Word is alive! Alive with faith, light, and power!"

Addy spoke, "God is Spirit. Words are spirit! And God said, Let us make man in our image, after our likeness (Gen.1:26) And the Lord God formed man of the dust of the ground, and breathed into his nostrils the breath of life; and man became a living soul. (Gen 2:7). You are a spirit, you have a soul, and you live in a body!" More faith-filled words came forth from Addy.

Matthew was sober now. He took a long glance around the interior of this tree of wonder, he grabbed his head, and shook it, "I have been so stupid, so very, very stupid." Addy flew closer to Matthew, "My (God's) people are destroyed for lack of knowledge" (Hosea 4:6). More Faith bees showed up as she spoke the written Word of God! Every individual word bubble glowed with a supernatural brilliance that was as bright as the sun but didn't hurt your flesh eyes. Matthew brought his hands down from his head, "I want to know more, I want more, I need more, I need more of him more of his Word! I have never been this hungry for his word!"

Addy continued, "What do bees do outside this tree in the earth realm?"

"They pollinate to produce food for all to eat," Matthew stated.

Addy asked Matthew, "What do bees do in this realm that you are in now?"

"Ah...I think you are about to tell me," he said with a smile.

"We produce food for thought, words that bring faith and wisdom and nourishment to your soul and spirit. We want to help you tend to your garden and cross pollinate in your heartland to bring forth good fruit in you, that will flow out of you, and into your present life. This is by personal invitation only. You are in control of how far you want to go, because 'faith without works is dead' (James 2:26). We will not do everything for you. Just as you spoke unpleasant words in this tree, our worker bees cleaned it up because you are the visitor, and we were showing you how we operate. We live by the Golden Rule. Do unto others as you would want them to do unto you!" (Matt. 7:12) Addy advised.

Matthew asked, "I am very sorry about what I said earlier, but how do I get to my garden in my soul?"

"First, if you want to do this, I need a yes or a no! This is a secret passage, only for those who have invited Jesus into their hearts can enter in because they have the Word of Faith key access." Addy was serious. Matthew made a long pause.

"I don't like my life outside of this tree. Not sure I like what is inside of me, but I like what I have seen, smelt, tasted, touched, and heard and what I have learned so far from Hope bringing me here. If I am inside of this tree now, because I invited Jesus into my heart while I was a kid at this camp years ago, then I do want to enter in deeper, because I don't regret entering into this tree! My answer Addy is yes!"

All of the Words filled with Faith within the tree shouted with joy and were dancing and buzzing about in celebration. Matthew was excited too. He also noticed that the Words of Faith that arrived with his voice inside moved around with him. They did not join the Words of Faith that Addy spoke earlier that moved around the tree. Matthew looked at Addy, and he could tell that she knew what he was thinking before he even said anything.

"Yes, Matthew! Those are your Words of Faith! They belong to you now. They will stay with you." Addy stated. "Are you ready to enter in?"

Matthew nodded yes! Addy flew up to a limb that was a little higher from where Matthew was sitting and pulled a few leaves off of his father's sun glasses. "We need to use these!" Matthew was instantly frozen in fear as if he were ten years old again. He was gasping. "Holy shhh (Beeeeep!)" He quickly threw his hand over his mouth, but it was too late! Angelic voices were singing, "Ah" was heard, and poop landed in front him as soon as he spoke the words!

The siren went off again and the soul patrol worker bees returned for another clean up. Matthew uncovered his mouth again and said, "Oops, I am so sorry about that!"

Addy gracefully said, "I know you are not used to having what you say as soon as you say it, but your words will find their way back to you eventually outside of this tree. Just because it doesn't happen as fast in the realm of time, they will show up at some point. Be not deceived. God is not mocked—for whatsoever a man soweth that shall he also reap" (Gal. 6:7).

Matthew had a flashback.

Sam asked, "Where are you going?"

Matthew answered, "To the baseball game."

Sam joked, "Hey, dude, don't get hit by a ball!"

Matthew returned, "Knowing my luck, I probably will!"

They both laughed.

Matthew was sitting in the crowd, watching the game, and the pitcher pitched the ball to the batter, and he hit a high fly. As the ball was in the air, he could now see his own words around the ball in the air directing the ball to himself, sitting in the stands. With a bird's eye view, he could see himself sitting in the crowd with a white and red hat that looked like a bulls eye target. Matthew looked up, smack, right in his eye.

Matthew said, "I am starting to see that is very true!"

He looked back up and pointed to his dad's glasses with some fear in his voice. "Where did those come from?"

Addy said, "They have been here since that summer in church camp."

"Since camp?" Matthew was feeling sick and he grabbed his head, "I don't know what's going on around here. I must have drank too much or had some really bad beer!"

Addy responded, "I know this is not easy, Matthew, but trust me, you will see more clearly and gain understanding. These glasses are the first step!"

Matthew was still stressing, "What do my dad's screwed up glasses have to do with anything? How am I going to see more clearly with those? They are backward!"

The reflective lenses were popped out and put in backward. The reflective side was now on the inside. Assuredly, Addy looked at the glasses and said, "They will work well for you just the way they are. Please take them! They will help you see your soul."

Reluctantly, Matthew reached for them and took them down off of the branch but held them away from himself like if he brought them in too close they might sting him. "This doesn't make any sense to me! And how are these supposed to help me see better?" Matthew stated.

Addy calmly and motherly, asked, "Have you ever heard that your eyes are the windows to you soul?"

"Yes, so?" Matthew said restlessly. "When you put those glasses on, you will be able to get a look inside your eye windows and see what I am talking about."

Matthew was sweating and clearly not amused by what Addy was asking him to do. Just touching his now dead father's glasses, unearthed a deep buried secret that was resurrecting to haunt him again. Addy could sense that a raw heart string had been played and had Matthew vibrating in childlike fear. He was not enjoying the act of touching the glasses and didn't want to add looking at them at the same time too.

Matthew's personal voiced Faith filled written Word of God bubbles, gathered together and gracefully rested as a group on the hand that was holding the damaged glasses. He was looking at Addy and was unaware that the Faith filled words were there. Matthew had calmed down and was breathing normal again.

"Have you ever been to a drive thru bank window?" she asked.

"Of course!" Matthew replied.

Addy continued to explain, "To make a deposit, you put your currency into the capsule and send it in. You instruct what your will wants done, with what you put in the container."

"Okay!" Matthew nodded.

Addy said, "Same with a word. Words are containers. Your intention (good or bad) and your attitude (good or bad) are blown into each word as a seed. Like blowing your breathe into a balloon, it is now shaped by a part of you, and it can now do something that it couldn't do before you filled it. It can carry the seed inside to a designated destination."

Addy paused for a brief moment before she asked him the next question.

"So Matthew, are you ready to take this secret trip inside of you?" Addy asked.

"I am not sure I can do this," Matthew said while he still was not looking at his father's glasses that he was holding.

Addy assured, "You do not have to make this trip alone. Hope is here now with your invisible glimmers. I will go too, and of course, no one can enter in without Faith! Speak out a word container, and Hope and I will get inside it and ride the word container in as you are hearing."

Matthew asked, "Am I dreaming? Because this makes no sense!"

Addy corrected him, "You mean earthly sense or cents that you deposit and buy stuff with? Then no, this is a journey into your soul, and the transportation and ticket into your heartland is the faith in words. It is not cars or trains made of steel, but the dimension of imagination and into the core of your being that only the Word of God can rightly divide you so you may see better."

Matthew was running out of excuses to delay the trip that he had said yes to.

Addy said, "Say 'word container!'"

Matthew said, "Word container!"

Instantly, it appeared in front of him, and it looked like a bank container at a drive thru bank. Addy opened the Word, Hope and Addy got in it, and Addy closed the Word.

Addy instructed, "Put on the glasses, close your eyes if you need to, until Faith, Hope, and I ride in the Words as you hear them. When you open your eyes, we will be on the inside of your windows to your soul. Now speak. You may enter in by Faith!"

Matthew closed his eyes, brought the glasses up to his face, put them on, and said, "You may enter in by Faith!"

As Matthew spoke those words and was hearing them, Faith lead the way in along with all of the Faith Words that had Matthew's voice inside. Addy and Hope followed in the spoken Word container.

It looked much like the internal workings of a drive thru bank. Just before the Faith bees arrived inside Matthew's head, the word

FAITH COMES BY HEARING

capsule—that Addy and Hope rode in—came to a halt in the slot just inside Matthew's flesh ears. Hope caught a glimpse of a child-like figure that fled from the control panel and disappeared through a door on the floor. Addy opened the word container and Hope, and she got out onto the control panel counter of the control room. Matthew opened his eyes.

The view that Faith, Addy, and Hope had from the control room were from the inside of Matthew's eye windows with his flesh eyes reflecting off of the mirrored side of his father's glasses. Addy and Faith flew up to the windows to get eye contact with Matthew. "Can you see us okay?" Addy asked.

Matthew quickly took off the glasses to examine them to see if they had some supernatural power to them. He turned them around and looked through the lens the way they were originally designed when his dad wore them, and then he put them back on his face.

"Whoa! I am amazed! It's like looking into yet another dimension. How is this happening?" Matthew asked.

Addy said, "It is happening by Faith, Matthew, in order for this to work properly"

Meanwhile, at the same time, as Addy was continuing this conversation with Matthew, Hope wandered off on her own.

CHAPTER 6

Control Room

Hope noticed a stained rug on the control room floor. It was covering a door on the floor that would not close because of an old vine that had grown up from the underside of Matthew's Heartland.

Addy and Matthew were still talking in the background.

Hope's curiosity led her to the door in the floor. She saw the childlike figure go down through the opening, so she leaned over, stretching as far as she could to see who it was. As she did, she fell right through the gap in the door on the floor. She started screaming, at least she was aware of it, but she noticed that her voice did not echo. It was like she was on mute, and even though she was falling, it was more like a downward pull into this dark place. She passed a dimly lit chandelier that had a few faint flames that were flickering on it. Hope whispered to herself, *Are those glimmers?* as she continued to descend deeper and deeper and landed into some creepy vines and weeds.

Hope whispered, "Where am I?" From this murky disturbing pile of over growth, Hope was trying to figure out precisely where she was. Looking out from her location, she saw a sign with flashing lights, and she blinked her eyes, making sure she was seeing correctly.

Theater of Mind…Now showing "TOXIC FOREST"
Starring…Self-Willie!

The "Self-Willie" part of the sign was lit up in individual lights that were blinking.

This sign was tied up with jump rope, and it was hanging between two thorny trees. The door to the theater looked like a huge mouth. There was a ticket booth in front of the theater that looked like a hollowed out dead tree trunk.

Hope was unfamiliar with this off beat landscape she had arrived at. She knew she was inside Matthew's Heartland, but I don't think she was expecting this. Hope knew she was lost without Faith, and she wasn't sure how to find her at this point either. Hope decided to check things out—she felt somewhat like an invisible and mute observer. She walked along the edges of this parched and almost colorless space, and she kept herself from blinking because she didn't want to be noticed at this point. Hope was used to collecting glimmers, but so far she was not seeing anything even close or worthy of keeping.

Hope heard someone coming. A young boy walked up to the ticket booth. Up popped a short man inside of the ticket booth, "Well hello! My name is Dean, Dean Nile. Welcome to Theater of Mind. Today's feature is 'TOXIC FOREST,' starring Self-Willie!"

Mr. Nile was dressed as a gypsy and rubbing a dirty crystal ball, full of black word currency. He said, "What's your name, sonny?"

The young boy said, "Daniel."

"How many tickets do you need today?" Mr. Nile asked.

Daniel answered, "Just one, but I don't have any money."

Mr. Nile, "No problem! We don't use money here, just words!"

Daniel said, "Really?!"

Mr. Nile replied, "Well, if you want to enter in, all you have to do is say the passwords, and you can get in!"

"Wow! So what do I have to say to get in?" Daniel asked.

Mr. Nile pulled out a ticket from the dirty crystal ball and pushed the ticket through the window hole. "That's all you have to say!"

Daniel said, "That's easy. I say this all the time!"

"Or"—Mr. Nile pulled out one more ticket—"if you say this, you can have the VIP pass, all inclusive, refreshments, backstage pass, and you will get to dine with the superstar of the show during the intermission. You can order anything you want." Mr. Nile slid the ticket through the window hole with one dirty finger, "All you have to say is this!"

Daniel read the password to himself and even he scrunched his face on this, and looked back at Mr. Nile, "I am not sure I should be saying that."

Mr. Nile said, "Nothing is going to happen. Don't you want to see the show? You will get the VIP pass along with a photo shoot. Just say what is written on the ticket!"

By now, Hope was moving in a little closer and was wondering what was on the VIP ticket. Mr. Nile was drawing Daniel in with his index finger, "Now you can say that!"

Daniel just gave in and let it rip, "I want beepity beep, beep, beep, beep, beep!"

Hope instantly plugged her ears and closed her eyes!

When she opened them, Mr. Nile was dressed like a professional photographer. Daniel was in front of a dirty bed sheet that was being used for a backdrop for his photo shoot. As the shutter of the camera was clicking away, Daniel's ego was exploding as if Mr. Nile had doused rapid miracle grow on it. Mr. Nile presented Daniel with his VIP pass with his picture on it and put it on him like he just earned a gold medal of honor for his effort.

When Daniel looked up, he was ready for his red carpet walk of fame. The theater entrance looked like a huge mouth, and a long red tongue rolled out as the red carpet runway.

Now dressed in a tuxedo, Mr. Nile stood proudly and smiled as the announcer for Access Williehood. "Welcome, welcome Daniel Jones to Theater of Mind! So glad to have you with us tonight as our VIP guest on the red carpet for the premiere showing of 'TOXIC FOREST!' Be sure that you stop by the concession stand and pick up anything that your little heart desires. We have a bunch of free samples!" Daniel walked through the big mouth doorway into the concession stand and large teeth came together closing the door to the entrance. He was greeted by forked and round shaped tongues, and as they walked about, they left slimy slobber in their wake. They were all babbling and hissing at Daniel as they asked him what he would like to order.

Mr. Nile was now dressed as the waiter with a soiled snot rag laid over his arm. He walked up to Daniel, holding a rusty tray of various samples in dirty, used paper cups, tuna, and sardine cans.

Mr. Nile asked, "Would you like some free samples? We have some 'Pain in the Necks,' 'Good for Nuthins,' 'Drive Me Nuts,' 'Sick N' Tireds,' 'Stupids,' and if you prefer we have some 'Damits,' or 'I'll be Damned.' Of course, we have 'Scared to Deaths,' 'FMLs,' 'FUs,' 'Skitzos,' 'Curse-itz,' and one of the most favorites, 'WTFs,' and 'Ur Killin Me's.' You can have it just like your father or mother did. All you have to do is pick it up with your mouth and say it! Like father, like son. Like mother, like daughter. You can have some depression, fear and high anxiety, alcoholism, drug addiction, sexual addiction, and the list goes on and on, but just so you know, it is all free, free, free! Try it, you'll like! Just have it your way!"

Hope was looking into the showcase that would normally be candies and popcorn and such. She could hardly believe this bizarre place. The aroma in this room was getting worse as the waiter was speaking. Hope was holding her nose and was looking for the nearest exit, and it was even making her stomach turn.

Daniel put his hand up and said, "No thanks! I am really not hungry!" He was looking for the entrance to the next part of the theater, he was anxious to go sit down.

As Daniel walked into the dimly lit theater and started to look for the best seat in the house, Hope noticed a small room at the top on the back wall with a flickering light coming through it. Hope whispered, "Ooo glimmers?" She flew up and peeked through the window and saw a weird image for a movie projector. It was Matthew's chest and heart projecting onto the movie screen.

Hope was thinking out loud, "For out of the abundance of the heart, your mouth speaketh. For as he thinketh, so is he" (Matt. 12:34; Prov. 23:7) She paused and started blinking, "Wow." It was like she had peeked around the curtain and found the Wizard of Oz running the show.

Interrupting her discovery, Mr. Nile entered the theater dressed as an usher. Pointing his flashlight into Daniel's face, he said, "The show is about to start. Please take your assigned seat." Mr. Nile seemed to be getting upset because most of his guests were not sitting were he wanted them to. He went from person to person, checking their tickets to make sure they were in their assigned seats.

The guests were everyone in Matthew's life who had offended or hurt his feelings in some way or another. Some people had doubles of themselves at different ages. Such as young Daniel and older Daniel, young Phyllis and older Phyllis, Bruce (his dad), sisters, teachers, classmates, coworkers, old girlfriends, ex-wife, and the lovers she cheated with. Anyone Matthew had conflict with at some point or another was in the theater. It was a packed house.

Some commotion occurred due to the guests not moving fast enough for Mr. Nile. He was getting edgier by the second. Just as the movie introduction started, loud noises ensued and a lit sign above the screen came down, saying, "Train of thought!" Instantly, the theater transformed into a passenger train car.

The lights then brightened, and Mr. Nile was now dressed as a train conductor. "Please be sure that you are all seated before the train takes off." Everyone was sitting down, and then up popped armrests at every seat. Jump ropes had come out of nowhere and wrapped themselves around each person's arms and legs, making them all hostages held captive on this train car.

By this time, Hope was down under a seat on the train. Mr. Nile started walking up and down the center isle of the car making sure that everyone was strapped in tightly. Dean Nile didn't see her, but even Hope was tied down by the fringe on the end of one of the jump ropes. Her eyes grew wide as the train car jerked, and it started to slowly move forward.

Mr. Dean Nile was standing outside the train of thought and now was dressed as the roller coaster operator, setting the speed dial for the ride. The train of thought engine was revving up for takeoff. Mr. Nile pressed the turbo button and the train blasted off like lightening. Frantic screams were heard. The train was on a wild coaster ride, with many twists and turns, extreme high peaks, and drastic descents that would make anyone sick. Mr. Nile just stood there with a devilish smile of satisfaction.

After a desirable and fulfilling length of time, the train of thought came to a sudden halt. Everyone's hair was messed up, and there was vomit everywhere. While the passengers were trying to gather their bearings, a marching band was heard. All the passengers on the train turned their heads in that direction. A parade was in the path in front of them, and Mr. Nile was the master of ceremonies. He was riding on this massive float of honor. From the blurry crowd, worship erupted with the casting of flowers, roses, gold coins, and paper money as they were heaped upon Mr. Nile.

He stood up and bowed, blowing kisses into the air, and he also kissed his fingers and placed them on his own cheeks while saying, "Thank you, thank you, thank you! I know, I am wonderful! It is all about me, me. Me, myself, and I!"

Behind him was a huge score board being pulled by the float he was on. On the scoreboard were various listings of his grudges, of those that he got even with, and how many times he got "his way."

The parade led up the path to a boxing ring, and Mr. Nile stepped off his float of honor onto Matthew's stained childhood bedroom rug. As he did so, he was wearing a silk robe, boxer shorts, and boxing gloves. The rug lifted him up and floated him over to the center of the boxing ring and majestically lowered him there.

Mr. Nile stepped off of the rug; and a referee walked over to him, bowed, kissed his feet, then stood with his microphone, and said, "Let's get ready to R-U-M-B-L-E. I'll show you!"

Behind the boxing ring, the scoreboard was displayed. One by one, the riders on the train of thought were released, and they mindlessly walked up into the ring one at a time. Mr. Nile punched them out with one single hit, and the scoreboard would register each knock out punch *win*, like a Vegas slot machine, registering the jackpot winner over and over and over and over.

Hope stayed on the train car but was still hiding under one of the seats. She was released the same time that the passengers were but was not called forth to enter the boxing ring like the others. Hope was not blinking, and there was nothing to be blinking about.

The train of thought had moved to the next location of toxic forest where there was a huge black cauldron boiling and brewing over a hot blazing fire in the dreary opening of the forest. Short Mr. Nile was dressed like a dark wizard/warlock stirring the cauldron with a large paddle.

Now, every passenger was standing on their own pedestal, while Mr. Dean Nile was stirring his pot of magic spells. The cauldron fumes burped images of his intent as he stabbed a Voodoo doll in the back while each one reacted to the pain.

Hope was still hiding on the train of thought, she didn't know what to do without Faith. She kept watching and didn't let herself blink, not even once. She was ready for this premiere to be over with.

Every guest looked sad, sick and weak and they were all sitting on odd looking benches. In one swift moment of grandeur, Mr. Nile spun a master handle and the benches they were sitting in, became vices... 'Vices of shame!' Mr. Nile shouted, "None of you should have messed with me. (evil laugh) Haha."

The train was in motion again, then came to another designated stop. There was a large crowd of mourners that were gathered around a certain man, and Mr. Nile was now dressed as the funeral director. He went up to this man and told him, "It is time to go now. Say your goodbyes, it is time!" The man that he was talking to turned around, slowly walked to the casket, and laid down in it.

The guests were starting to cry. Hope could not see who Mr. Nile ordered to get into the casket. The crowd was in the way, and she started running through the mourners. She tried and tried to make her way through the crowd. So, she decided to fly so she could see. Her mouth dropped open, and her eyes could hardly believe it. It was grown up Matthew! The scene faded to darkness.

The lights came back on in the train of thought, and Mr. Nile was dressed as the train conductor, looking at Daniel Jones. He was the only one left on the train, except Hope, who was still the mute observer.

Mr. Nile said, "Intermission. Well, Daniel"—the age that Daniel was at church camp—"I see you are the only one this evening that has the VIP pass. I would like to escort you to the café car so you may dine with the star of the show. This way, please." He was pointing to the exit.

Daniel was seated at a table in the café car. Mr. Nile walked in dressed as the waiter again with the snot infested rag over his arm while carrying a plate. "Here ya go, Daniel, this is what you ordered. Enjoy every bite!"

Daniel looked at his plate and realized the words that he said to get the VIP pass, and he started to gag. Hope could not take it anymore, and she darted out of the café car, flew through toxic forest as fast as she could fly, up past the chandelier, and up through the door in the floor and into the control room.

Addy and Matthew were still on the same sentence when she re-entered the control room.

Addy continued, "I need you to leave the glasses on and focus for a bit."

Matthew said, "I can't do this right now. This is more than I can handle."

"We can try this later if you would like," Addy replied.

"I would like that Addy. I am not feeling well," Matthew admitted.

Addy looked at Hope and said, "Are you okay?"

Hope looked strange and not herself. "No, I don't think I can do this right now either."

Addy said, "You are going to have to speak us out of here, Matthew!"

Matthew cleared his throat and the control room rumbled. Hope was knocked over by it, but she got back up and dusted herself off. Addy and Hope got back in the word container and closed it. Matthew said, "You may exit!"

Addy and Hope rode the word container out of his mouth and Faith followed. Everyone was back in the tree.

Matthew was confused. "Sorry! I am really sorry! This all was making me dizzy."

Addy said, "It's okay, Matthew, but I want you to see that you are really on a treasure hunt!"

"Treasurer hunt?" Matthew replied. "What treasure?"

"The treasure inside you!" Addy informed.

Matthew said, "I really don't understand your riddle!"

Addy calmly stated, "You are stuck, Matthew. Stuck where you got hurt!"

Hope shook herself, like a chill went down her spin, and said in a whisper, "He is more than stuck!" Hope did a small gag just thinking about the nightmare trip she just went on. For the first time, Hope looked sad and confused by this twisted display, or should she really call it a twisted production, twisted play, or script coming from Matthew's heart.

"I am stuck where I got hurt?" Matthew asked.

Addy replied, "Yes, and that is where your treasure is!"

Matthew sarcastically spouted, "My treasure is in my pain? Are you kidding me?"

Addy humbly said, "Yes, Matthew, if you go to your pain, that is where your treasure is!"

Matthew looked more confused than ever, and the Soul Patrol bees gathered around him and started singing this song:

50 Ways to Leave Your Lover
Paul Simon
THERE IS A KEY!

> The problem is all inside your heart
> Can't you see
> The answer is easy if you
> Take it logically
> We can help you with your struggle
> To be free
> There is a decision key
> To change your Heartland
>
> It's really not our habit
> To intrude
> Furthermore, His Word
> Will not be lost or misconstrued
> But we'll repeat ourselves

At the risk of being rude
There is a key
To change your Heartland
A key to change your Heartland

Chorus: repeat 2x

First, don't play the "Blame Game"
Make a new plan, man
Put away the toys, boy
To set yourself free
Get off the "Cuss Bus"
You don't need to fuss much
Just pick up the D key
And set yourself free

We say it grieves us so
To see you in such pain
We know there is something you could do
To make you smile again
We appreciate that You need us to explain
About the Decision key

Why don't we all
Just sleep on it tonight
And in the morning
You'll begin to see the light
So we'll see you then
And realize we are probably right
There is a key
To change your Heartland
Decision key to change your Heartland

Matthew seemed to calm down some after the Soul Patrol sang to him about the decision key, but Matthew was running the train of thought even though he didn't know Hope was there too. Hope was deferred and it made her heart sick at what she saw. Hope was helpless inside Matthew without Faith by her side. She was tired and spent, and she curled up under a leaf and took a nap.

Matthew didn't feel right either, it was obvious that his Heartland was not a happy place, and he too needed to relax a bit. He rested his head on a branch and closed his eyes.

Matthew had another flash back dream of church camp 1966:

The white tabernacle of Heartland Camp was a tall wide building with open rafters and side paneled doors all the way around the building that lifted up onto poles. It was open and airy except for the part behind a large stage. There was a podium, piano, and seats for a choir, and in front of the stage was an altar.

Matthew had his guitar, and Marcus was standing with him on the right side of the stage. They were practicing a song to sing together for the talent show.

A group of girls gathered along the outside of the tabernacle, watching the boys practice. Millie and Betty (Matthew's sisters) could see Phyllis walking across the lawn with her clipboard just waiting to catch someone out of line 'in her book'.

Phyllis stopped as she heard Matthew and Marcus singing, and the girls could see her glaring with jealousy at how good they were. Phyllis adjusted her cat-eyed glasses and started hot footing it to the next thing on her list. Matthew's sisters witnessed her spite and gathered all the girls around them and began their jump roping routine as soon as Phyllis was out of sight. Millie said, "Wait! I gotta good one!"

Betty and Sally started swinging the jump rope round and round, and Millie hopped in, chanting:

> She's making her list
> Checking it twice
> You're gonna find out
> She's really not nice
> Phyllis Jones is snooping through town
>
> She pushes around poor Carl
> She blames him for her mistakes

She preaches about her 'morals'
But we all know she's a fake!

You better watch out
It's all a big lie
She goes to church
But we don't know why
Phyllis rides her broomstick through town.

The girls gathered in a circle laughing hysterically and agreeing at the truth of the chant and begin clapping. Meanwhile, Daniel came in and sat down at the piano and played a few bars loudly to get everyone's attention. He swayed his head back and forth acting like Ray Charles while wearing Bruce's glasses and started singing... "Hit the road Matt, and don't you come back no more, no more, no more, no more Hit the road Matt, and don't you come back no more."

Matthew's mouth dropped open as soon as he noticed that Daniel was wearing his dad's glasses with the lens popped out and put in backward. Matthew tossed down his guitar, which put a crack in it, and he started running toward Daniel. Matthew yelled, "I'm going to kill you, Daniel!"

Daniel darted off the stage, and Marcus followed right behind Matthew. Daniel ran out of the tabernacle, out onto the lawn, and headed over the bridge. Matthew was right on his heels. Daniel ran over to the big tree and darted around it a couple of times. As Matthew almost caught him, Daniel threw Bruce's glasses into the tree, and as he took one more step, Marcus tripped Daniel; and it made him trip and fall right into the water. All the children, watching from across the brook, started laughing and clapping.

A few moments later, Phyllis marched onto the scene to see what the commotion was, only to find her precious son in the water. Hysterically, Phyllis yelled, "Daniel. Daniel!" Daniel took one last look at Matthew, and Marcus, with a grin on his face, then turn toward his mother and started crying like he was hurt. Phyllis ran over the bridge to his rescue. Daniel started fake crying, "Mommy,

Matthew pushed me in. He's just afraid that I am going to beat him and Marcus out at the talent show."

Phyllis stepped down to the water's edge to help her son out of the water, saying stern and judgementally, "I knew that boy was up to no good! He is just like his father. Matthew, you should be ashamed of yourself, picking on Daniel just because you are jealous. I am pulling you out of the talent show. You and Marcus, both!"

Matthew heard echoes of Addy's voice...

"You are stuck, Matthew, stuck where you got hurt!" Pause.

"If you go to your pain, that is where your treasure is!" Pause.

"You are on a treasure hunt!"

Matthew slowly opened his eyes and saw that he was still in the tree, and Matthew's words of faith were still around him. Hope was resting on the toe of his shoe with her face propped in her front legs. Addy flew over to Matthew, and she welcomed him from his sleep.

She said, "Hello, Matthew, glad to see that you look rested. So, what have you decided about the decision key?"

Matthew looked down at Hope on his shoe, she was randomly blinking. "Will you show me where my glimmers are?" Hope started blinking a little faster, "I, Hope it to (pointing to Faith) be so! I will only go if Faith goes! I can't do anything without Faith!"

Matthew said, "And I can't go in without Hope or Faith because I clearly don't know the way!"

Addy spoke, "Amen, but remember. Thy word is a lamp unto my feet and a light unto my path. We need the light of his Word to guide us."

Matthew remembered, "Hey, that's in the Bible!"

Addy said, "Yes it is! And on this trip, you are going to see that most people are living their lives from the outside in, and it should be the other way around."

Matthew nodded, "I've heard that before, but—"

Faith said, "Well, we all want you to get off the playground and grow up."

"Ouch! Yes, I know that is truer than I want to admit." Matthew looked downward and was a little embarrassed. "I've decided to go in, but I want you all to go with me. My garden in my heart needs cross pollinated for sure."

Hope itched her antenna and whispered to herself, "Don't I know it! Geez."

CHAPTER 7

A Light unto My Path

Addy said, "Matthew, the Word created you, which the Word's name now is Jesus. God is spirit, and he breathed himself into man. Man is a spirit, and he has a soul and lives in a body here on earth. So, the only way to show you is to rightly divide you according to the written word. I want you to read this out loud, so you can bring forth more faith words filled with your voice inside them, not mine. Because faith comes by hearing and hearing by the word of God. When you hear yourself say his word, it changes you. It brings forth more faith to help cross pollinate your garden in your soul/heartland. Those faith-filled words belong to you because you blew a part of yourself into them, just like the Word blew a part of himself into mankind."

Addy flew to the core center of the tree and opened a hidden door, and Addy pulled out a beam of light and brought it to Matthew. It was of brilliant light matter that was bright as the sun but didn't burn his eyes. She handed it to Matthew, and as he took it, it unrolled in his hands like a scroll. It was like seeing living cells moving on a TV screen, these words were full of supernatural power, it was the written word of God.

Matthew was very reverent about holding these words and could even hear and feel faith current coming from them. Matthew looked at Addy, and she directed him to a passage—a "key" passage to help him enter in.

Matthew spoke:

> For the word of God is quick, and powerful, and
> sharper than any two-edged sword, piercing even
> to the dividing of soul and spirit, and joints and
> marrow, and is a discerner of the thoughts and
> intents of the heart. Neither is there any creature
> that is not manifest in his sight: but all things
> are naked and opened unto the eyes of him with
> whom we have to do.(Heb. 4:12–13)

Addy pointed to another verse.

Matthew read and spoke. "For thou wilt light my candle: the Lord my God will enlighten my darkness" (Ps. 18:28).

Addy pointed to another verse.

Matthew spoke, "He that getteth wisdom loveth his own soul, he that keepeth understanding shall find good" (Prov. 19:8)

With the sound of Matthew's voice, light, and matter, movement and power of faith was brought forth. More faith-filled words arrived, hovered, and joined the other faith words filled with Matthew's voice. Matthew didn't say another word, but he looked at the new faith-filled words that gathered around him like his own personal helpers.

Matthew was still holding the lit scroll of the written Word of God.

After a long pause, Matthew's eyes started to water, "For the first time in a long time, I feel love. Real unconditional love!" The words embraced Matthew. "No one is ever going to believe what is happening to me!"

Addy said, "It really doesn't matter what anyone else thinks or believes about you. It only matters what you believe about you, only you can change you! Faith in God's word is the only thing that pleases him."

Addy continued, "Words are seeds. His word is full of life and light, not death and darkness. Your soul/ heartland is like a garden full of spoken words from your entire life that came by hearing and you saying and hearing them. His written word says in Proverbs 18:21, 'Death and life are in the power of the tongue: and they that love it shall eat the fruit thereof.' God's words are true and meant for life, love, blessing, forgiveness, help, wisdom, freedom, hope, peace, instruction, healing, and strength. And a lot of negative worldly words came carelessly and on purpose to hurt, to lie about you, offend, enslave, curse, and deeply trouble you and bring doubt, sickness, fear, and hate, and then bring you to self-destruction."

Matthew said, "I have been slowly self-destructing my whole life, and I am tired of it!"

Addy asked, "Remember what brought you here to the camp?"

Matthew answered back, "No, I really don't know the answer to that."

"Your spirit man inside you brought you back to the place where you found new life, born again life. This is where your internal spirit man candle was lit, but this is also the place where the enemy tried to steal that new life out of you. That light still burns within you, it is still there."

Matthew looked at Addy like a light bulb came on, "I may have been drunk, but my spirit man wasn't!"

All of the faith-filled words that were in the tree cheered and danced about!

Addy said, "Absolutely! Correct! Most battles are on the inside of man, but you need to learn all three parts of you so you can win the battle within. You are already building your shield of faith. As more Faith comes so does strength."

Addy pointed to another verse.

Matthew spoke in Ephesians 6:16. "Above all, taking the shield of faith, wherewith ye shall be able to quench all the fiery darts of the wicked."

More faith-filled words appeared and added to Matthew's side. Matthew sat there stunned at the simplicity of gaining more faith, "I speak God's words and more faith comes."

Addy confirmed once again, "So then faith comes by hearing and hearing by the word of God, as said in Romans 10:17. You are calling it forth with your voice, you can't just read it or think it. Jesus called Lazarus from the dead, he didn't think him out of the grave."

Matthew said, "Wow, you are right! I never saw it this clearly before. The more I speak God's word to myself and hear them, more faith comes, and I am cross pollinated!"

All the faith-filled words danced about again as Matthew spoke. Hope was just as happy (and blinking) to see that he may be starting to think more clearly because she had no desire to ride his train of thought again!

The scroll rolled up on its own, and Matthew handed it to Addy, and she took it and put it back. Matthew looked at his faith shield growing, "I think I am ready to send you all in by hearing and hearing by the word of God!" Matthew smiled and winked.

Addy smiled back at him proudly, "Well let's get that word container here first for Hope and I to ride in. We will follow Faith."

Matthew said, "Word container!"

It arrived just as spoken. Hope and Addy got in and closed the hatch. Matthew closed his eyes, put on his father's backward glasses, and said, "Let's all enter in by Faith!"

As soon as the Faith words and the word container arrived inside the control room, a short shadow zipped off a stool and darted down through the open crack of the door in the floor to Matthew's heartland. Addy and Hope climbed out of the capsule, and she asked, "Can you see okay?"

Matthew blinked again. "What was that, or who was that?"

Addy said, "Good, you can see okay!"

Matthew asked again, "Who was that?"

Addy looked at Matthew through his eye windows and said, "You will find out soon enough, but if you want to go look now, I need to know if it is okay for me to open the door?"

He said, "Yes! I decide we all can enter in."

Addy pulled back the stained rug and opened the door in the floor. As the words of faith entered first through the door in the floor, their entrance gave new light into the corridor of his Heartland. As they moved passed the dimly lit chandelier that Hope saw before, it got much brighter. The vibration of currency and transference of energy happened on its own. The light of the word transferred to the chandelier, and the Faith bees were released into Matthew's heartland. Simultaneously, as this happened, the bees of faith spoke the written word.

> For thou wilt light my candle: the Lord my God
> will enlighten my darkness. (Ps. 18:28)

Matthew could now see clearly past the entrance and into his heartland because of the transfer of light. "Huh!" It clearly took his breath away for a moment. It almost felt like his dad's broken glasses were as virtual reality glasses into his soul. He was there just as the others were but not in body/flesh form.

Addy heard Matthew's huge inhale. "Are you okay?"

"Wow, this is a big head trip! This really isn't what I expected. It's like a dream, but I am awake. I feel limitless yet confined, very real but not logical. I am hearing my self talk, but my lips are not moving. You can hear me?"

Addy and Hope nodded their heads. Addy said, "Yes, we can hear you just fine. You have entered into layer two of you. The soul realm where the mind, will, and emotions part of you operate in."

Matthew was struggling with the idea or the reality in this layer of himself that he had to somehow control or filter his thoughts because they were for all to hear. Matthew was thinking out loud, *It is so dingy and colorless, parched, and like a drought down here. I must be a hot mess! I am really struggling here after being in the tree, and now I am here. I am having a hard time trying to control my train of thought because I don't want to offend my newfound friends. Sorry, but I feel like I need a drink, and I don't mean water.*

Addy said, "Calm down, you will be just fine. We need to take this one step at a time."

CHAPTER 8

Train of Thought

They all arrived at the theater of mind. Mr. Nile, the short little gypsy man standing in the ticket booth, streaked away like a shadow as soon as the Word of faith bees showed up. The gypsy costume fell to the ground. The Word of faith bees spoke in unison, "For rebellion is as the sin of witchcraft, and the stubbornness is as iniquity and idolatry. Because thou hast rejected the Word of the Lord, he hath also rejected thee from being king" (1 Sam. 15:23).

Matthew said, "Who was that?"

Addy said, "That was your self-manufactured personality."

Huh? Matthew thought. His thoughts broadcasted like live radio in this realm.

Addy continued, "Your constructed personality or you could call it your self-ego. Every human being has at least one."

Matthew asked, "How did he get inside me?"

Addy said factually, "You created him."

I what? Matthew was thinking loudly here.

Addy stopped in front of the ticket booth with the dirty crusty crystal ball and the costume on the floor. "You built him. Your sin nature started to construct him when you were very young. Your self-ego started to grow and develop when you figured out how to get your own way. Your self-willie will never mature beyond adolescence, but it will grow in power if it is not controlled. You could also call it your inner child gone wild."

Matthew said, "That was my self-will? That's embarrassing!"

Addy continued, "But this is not what your God given freewill started out as. That was a gift. This is something you made from your desires of selfishness. Self-willie wants what it wants, when it wants it, and will do anything and say anything to get its own way. If you don't learn to control it, it will take over and control all of you, your spirit, your soul, and your body!"

"Huh? I am not sure I understand."

Addy stated, "Self-willie hates *spirit* light that comes from the word of God. It is his kryptonite. He loves the darkness, so he can hide and do what he wants in secret. This is what you have created in you and allowed to grow in power without any discipline. Your self-willie is your worst enemy! This is not your parent's fault, and the blame game stops here. Sorry, but only you have yourself to blame, and only you can change it. The truth, and only the truth, will set you free. No amount of fame or money, booze or drugs, sex or stuff is going to fix this problem." She pointed to the parched cracked soil. "Your self-willie has hardened the soil of your heartland and caused all of this to die off".

Matthew was stunned by the decay and sad condition of his soulful real estate. His inner voice was speechless.

"Matthew, this is your Self-Willie starring in toxic forest. This is his twisted show that has been in production since you were a child and has been adding passengers to ride for years. It is a never-ending rerun that goes on and on and on. I think that it is time to enter in and pull the plug and set your soul free."

As the word of faith bees buzzed past the red-carpet tongue, it retracted, and the "Access Williehood" interviewer costume with microphone was laying lifeless on the hardened soil.

In unison, the word of faith bees spoke, and they flew around the microphone and empty lifeless costume, "Thou shall not go up and down as a talebearer among thy people: neither shalt thou stand against the blood of thy neighbor: I am the Lord" (Lev. 19:16).

Before the word of faith bees flew through the mouth door, the theater lights blew out on the Self-Willie sign. As they entered the concession stand, the slimy forked tongues were nowhere in sight, they had cleared out, and the waiter's outfit and tray were in a pile on the floor.

Word of faith bees spoke, "Death and life are in the power of the tongue, and they that love it shall eat the fruit there of" (Prov. 18:21).

Word of faith bees, Addy and Hope entered into the next room where there were now empty theater seats, and on the floor was the usher's costume and glowing wand still slightly flickering and then burned out. Hope was grateful that things were not the same as they were on her first trip through here.

Word of faith bees flew up to the projector room opening in the wall, the projector was stuck on pause, and the movie technician's clothes were on the floor. Word of faith bees voiced in unison, "For where your treasurer is, there will your heart be also. The light of the body is the eye: if therefore thine eye be single, the whole body shall be full of light. But if the eye be evil, thy whole body shall be full of darkness. If therefore the light that is in thee be darkness, how great is that darkness!" (Matt. 6:21–23).

When the bees flew down from the projector room, the theater was now the train of thought, and they flew to the front of the passenger rail car and buzzed off the train. Addy and Hope followed. Hope was more than delighted to see that the same creepy show was not playing again. She knew it was because faith was at work, chasing away fear and doubt that self-willie had brought into play over and over. For the first time in a long time, this train of thought was not in service and no tickets to ride were sold today. It was like a breeze of fresh air came through and lifted some of the toxic fog, causing Matthew to start freely thinking again. It was heard from the walls of his soul. "What is all this? A theater turned into a train? This is all inside me?"

Addy replied, "Matthew, this is your heartland/soul realm. Your mind (imagination) and emotions, plus your self-will operates here. This is housed inside your flesh, your earth suit."

"I feel so exposed, naked, and ashamed at having others inside me."

Matthew closed his eye lids and realized his view was more beyond doubt.

Addy responded, "You mean others inside you that you can't control?"

"I don't know if I can handle all this right now!"

Addy, with her wisdom, hit him head-on. "Only the truth will set you free! Stop running to another moment in time with the excuse that you can't handle it. You can set yourself free. It is your appointed time to break your denial, Mr. Dean Nile. Stop your self-destruction from going to another drink or drug, or into another dysfunctional relationship and blaming everyone else for it when you made most of this mess yourself!"

Matthew asked, "How do I do that? I really want and need your help here."

Addy answered, "You found Hope again and Faith bees are here to sow. What are you missing?"

Matthew thought, "Me? I? I hope so! I hope it to be so. I hope it to bee sow!"

"Yes!" Addy agreed. "Now all you need to find is your 'I'—self-willie. This is the works part that most everyone runs from. Like a child that trashes his room and doesn't want to clean up the mess that he made. It really takes more effort in running and hiding, lying and denying, than owning one's own sin."

"My self-willie, where do I look?" Matthew asked.

"You know, Matthew, think about why you reacted to the sight of your dad's glasses," Addy stated.

I can't stand the sight of these glasses, and I can't believe that I even put them on again! Matthew thought out loudly and began to notice a tone to his soul's voice that didn't sound as mature as he did earlier.

Matthew cleared his throat and said, "Wow, it's getting warm in here!"

Addy said, "Yes, your emotions are starting to run hot!"

What does that mean?" Matthew said.

"I think you really already know, Matthew! I mentioned your dad's glasses, and now it's hot in here," Addy said.

"My dad was a mean SOB. He made our life a living hell!"

"Ah, ah…," Matthew grunted.

He had a long pause. "That was me. Self-willie me!"

"Yes!" Addy approved. "Your first breakthrough in exposing your denial—your Dean Nile! You are already learning to rightly divide yourself and hear the difference within."

"I heard my self-willie, but where is it?"

Addy asked, "Well, your self-willie is the immature child in you that is always playing hide and seek, never wants to be found out, loves the blame game, and never likes to be disciplined or corrected."

So what do I do with that? Matthew thought, as his inner voice came through loud and clear.

"Who do you put on your train of thought every day or when you feel like running it?" Addy asked.

"All the people I can't stand!" Willie took over the soul speaker again. *This is like a switch, going off and on in me, and I don't know how this is happening,* Matthew thought.

Addy said, "Let's think back to where this all originally started. When Adam was created, Adam wasn't even aware that he was naked in his flesh because he was totally God conscience in the Garden of Eden. He was living and communing at the highest level on earth, which was God's original plan. Lucifer was a beautiful angel in heaven that became jealous of God and wanted to be worshiped and exalted above God. It got himself and a third of the angels cast out of heaven and onto the earth. He was already here before Adam and Eve were created. He was the serpent that slithered in, lied, and tricked Eve into eating the forbidden fruit of the tree of knowledge of good and evil."

"That's right, it was all Adam and Eve's fault that we are all in this mess!" Matthew's snotty self-willie voice took over again. Matthew was shocked to hear the difference in the voice tone and immaturity of himself. He cleared his throat again, but he could not control his inner voice sound waves, vibrating though his soul, and the thermostat changes that came with it.

Addy did not respond to Self-willie's comment, but she kept on sowing wisdom into the situation. "The serpent wanted to break Adam and Eve away from God consciousness and into a lower level of thinking and being. Self-consciousness steered man way from God-consciousness. The obsession of self is what got Lucifer kicked out of heaven. He couldn't stand seeing the beauty of what God had created for mankind and how much God enjoyed and loved them. Satan's jealousy and hatred for God made him want to rip man from loving God and being close with him. Satan, the father of all lies, continued lying and tricking them into serving themselves and believing that they could become like God. Being self-conscious and prideful is the biggest problem mankind has to this day."

Matthew said, "I can't believe I am this age, and I am just now seeing the truth about this stuff!"

Addy responded, "I am sure at one time or another, you heard or read something on this subject, but the enemy came and stole the words of wisdom from you before they had a chance to take root in you. Adam and Eve never had parents but God. They never were children. From that point on, everyone was raised by fallen humans. Satan knows that children are vulnerable and defenseless, so he goes to work early in destroying trust and makes them adolescent victims that will one-day turn their hurts and hates into destructive volunteers. Either they will destroy themselves or they will destroy others that try to get in their way."

Matthew thought, "It's like hurting children that are still operating in adult bodies that are now hurting their own children with their issues!"

Addy said, "Yes! And that is how a generation curse is passed on and on and on, until someone finds the truth and changes it. A blessing that can be carried for a 1,000 generations! 'He sent his word, and healed them, and delivered them from their destructions'" (Ps. 107:20).

Matthew said, "I never even took the time or considered to look inside myself. It was always so much easier blaming the next guy."

Addy replied, "That's because you and your self-willie have been running on auto pilot for years and years, and this is your appointed time to make your choice. Destroy your self and others in your path and do it your way, or do it God's way."

Matthew stated, "I do want to change! It really is ridiculous having a spoiled rotten adolescent run my life."

Addy agreed. "Here is where the work begins. It is a battle that goes on every minute of every day and night, even in your sleep. Your self-willie will try to hijack your train of thought at any given moment, but you are the only one that holds the key to switch your track on him!"

"So, Addy, where do I find self-willie?" Matthew thought.

Addy repeated, "I told you before, go to your pain, that is where your treasure is!"

"What? I want to find my self-willie, not revisit pain in my life!" Matthew was feeling hot again.

Addy paused a moment because she noticed the fog was getting thick again and Matthew's breathing was short and tense. Addy spoke anyways, "If you don't forgive your father, God can never bless you!

"What?" Self-willie's voice came through loud and clear. "That jerk never said he was sorry! He made our lives a living hell. He used to smack my mom around, break things, and drank every chance he could get. He ran my friends off. I never wanted to bring them to our house because I never knew how he was going to act!"

Toxic fog rolled in even thicker, but Addy was not affected or impacted by it. She was protected by an invisible shield round about her in this atmosphere. Addy called, "Matthew! Do you hear me? Breathe slowly and calm down!"

Matthew started to do what she said, and the toxic fog subsided and backed off some.

Addy continued, "You are in the battlefield for your mind. Self-willie wants to control your train and your control panel! If he has control of your 'train of thought,' it will be fueled with his toxic anger and revenge, which will ultimately crash and burn you and all those who try to love you!"

Matthew took another forced breath and a little more fog lifted, "I feel so stuck and confined like I can't even move?"

Hope started blinking. "Wait, I think I know why!"

Matthew said, "Why?"

Hope got excited and was blinking wildly. "I saw self-willie's show!"

Matthew returned, "What? How?"

Hope started flying about and lighting up the place. "I got it. I got it. I think you are buried some place in your Heartland!"

Matthew laughed, "My hope chest is buried in my Heartland not me!"

Hope said, "Yes, yes, you are! I saw your funeral!"

Matthew was louder this time. "What the heck are you talking about?"

Addy said, "Hold on Matthew, let Hope speak."

Hope continued, "When we came into Matthew's control room the first time, I saw a shadow of a child streak down the door in the floor. I was curious and peeked through the door in the floor to see who it was, and I also saw some flickering lights and I thought they might be glimmers. I must have leaned over too far. I thought I was falling, but I was being pulled downward into Matthew's heartland. To make a long story short, I saw self-willie's show and took an unexpected trip on his 'train of thought.' One of the train stops in toxic forest was at a funeral, and self-willie was playing Mr. Nile. He was dressed as the funeral director and told adult Matthew it was time to go. Self-willie commanded Matthew to say goodbye to everyone as he crawled in the casket, then the scene went black. I really think self-willie/Mr. Nile may have been suspicious that someone else was watching. I bet he buried Matthew's soul somewhere in here, and that's why the scene ended at the funeral instead of the graveyard."

Matthew fired back, "This is crazy, how could he bury my soul?"

Addy answered, "As a form of control! He can't kill your soul, but he could confine your soul by taking your power away from you!"

Hope said, "Or you giving it to him!"

Matthew said, "How could he do that?"

Addy said, "He's wearing you down just like a child would a parent. Temper tantrum after temper tantrum, moment after moment, day after day, year after year, thought after thought. It's all about me, me, me, and it's mine, mine, mine. You have submitted your soul (mind, will, and emotions) to your own bully, self-willie, and he is now holding your soul hostage. You have not made your self-willie submit to any laws or commandments of what your soul feels and your spirit knows! Self-willie is an immature child in you that needs parented 24/7, guided, nurtured, and made to submit to boundaries of what is right and wrong. You cannot kill your self-willie, but you can kill its power and control over you. The truth is prisons are full of self-willies that have over ridden the souls of the people they dwell in. They were hurt, and they wanted revenge on anyone and anything that came across their paths. It is the self destructive nature in a man (self-will) that could have been controlled and made to abide by the law of right and wrong, by the spirit and the soul from the inside, but now they are controlled from the outside in and caused the whole man (spirit-soul-body) to sit behind bars!"

"Oh my gosh, I think you are right!" Matthew said sadly. "I feel so constricted and squeezed, but I don't feel that way in my flesh. I think I can finally tell the difference between the two. So you are saying that we are looking for my soul and not for my self-willie?"

"Yes, you are right!" Addy said.

"Where do we start looking?" Matthew said.

"Well, the best place to start is, we have to think like a child" Addy said. "More like out of sight, out of mind."

Hope chimed in, "By the looks of the hard dry land around here, he has to be close to the surface!"

Addy replied, "Good point!"

Matthew said sadly, "I hope I don't regret—"

Hope cut him off, "That's it! That's it!"

Matthew said, "What's it?"

Hope was blinking a lot again, "That's it! You have not had any glimmers for me to collect lately, in fact, not in quite sometime because you are in regret!"

Matthew said, "What's that supposed to mean?"

Hope was so excited to be on this clue hunt with them, "You are stuck in regret, your soul is in regret!"

Addy said, "Good job, Hope! I think you are onto something!"

Hope said, "If self-willie had a funeral for you, you are probably buried in the valley of regret!"

"The valley of regret? What is that?" Matthew asked.

Hope said, "It has to be a grave yard!"

"In here? In me?" Matthew said.

Addy said, "Of course! This in your mind, imagination's train of thought that runs and travels in this inner world that is not earthly but has symbolic similarities of it's nature."

Hope said, "We need to follow your train tracks, and I know we will find the grave yard of regrets."

CHAPTER 9

Rivers of Living Water

They were off the train and followed the tracks to where the roller coaster started. Hope said, "No way am I gonna do this ride again, I am gonna fly, thank you very much! I think we all should."

They all bypassed the crazy coaster track and found the end of the ride. They saw the left overs of the *me* parade, the float with costumes, lying lifeless, and a scoreboard that was unplugged at the moment. Matthew's dirty carpet was lying in the center of the boxing ring with empty boxing shorts on top.

They continued to follow the tracks into the toxic forest where a black cauldron stopped bubbling its vile contempt, and dead black words had turned into lumps of porous lifeless rocks. Many empty pedestals encircled the cauldron, and a voodoo doll was lying on the ground next to Mr. Nile's sorcerer costume. The ironic part of this was that the pin was stuck in the sorcerer's cape. They continued down the tracks to the empty benches that turned into the vices of shame, and then the tracks lead them to the next location in toxic forest, the funeral parlor.

No one was there except Mr. Nile's suit and tie on the floor. Hope said, "This is where the scene went black. When I tried to see who got in the casket, I flew up because everyone was in my way, and I couldn't see. That has to be when self-willie saw me and noticed someone else was here."

Addy said, "I think if we follow the tracks from here, the grave yard has to be next!"

Matthew went quiet, but Addy, Hope, and Faith bees moved on down the tracks. This track seemed well traveled through toxic forest, and it looked like it took many trips round and round what seemed to be a three-ring circle of chaos. The trees were so dark and prickly, and the thorns were dripping with black sticky bile.

They continued down the track into a dark valley. There it was, the gate to the cemetery, "Valley of Regret." Many tombstones were erected for a million different things—lost games, destroyed dreams, dead pets, broken toys, failed tests, lost friendships, failed jobs, failed relationship with dad, divorce, and failed relationships with children—the lot was full. But right in the center was a funeral tent that was set up over a dark shallow hole.

Gasping was heard. They all flew to the funeral tent, but Hope went under it.

Hope blinked, so she could see better, and shouted, "Matthew, it's you!"

Matthew's soul was tightly confined by the hardened soil of the shallow grave. His soul was gasping silently and could not get up.

Hope started to panic, "How do we help him?"

Addy said, "We can't!"

Matthew's inner voice spoke up again, "Why not?"

Addy said, "Your self-willie put you here, and you let him do this to you."

Matthew said, "So, what can I do?"

Addy encouraged him, "You have to loosen the soil of your soul/heartland dirt."

Matthew said, "So, where do I find a shovel that will work in here?"

Addy replied, "A shovel will not help. You need water to loosen your soil."

"Oh, I need to drink some water, of course!" Matthew said.

"Wrong!" Addy said. "Wrong department again. Rightly divide yourself!"

"Oh right! Flesh needs H20 water. Soul needs words," Matthew said. "But how do I get water in my soul soil?"

"Rightly divide, Matthew, think," Addy encouraged.

"Water comes from wells, of course mine are dry. Words are for soul realm. Word is God. God is spirit The women at the well met Jesus and received living water. God's Word is living water to my soul!" Matthew said.

Addy said, "Absolutely! You know enough truth to set yourself free. Words have seed in them. God's Words have faith, seed, water, and power! I know you are stuck, but you can still think and speak from what you already have planted in you. You need to be still and listen. Shh. Listen, listen from the good roots that are deep within you from the core of your soil being."

Addy, Hope, and Matthew's word of faith bees landed upon Matthew's tombstone, so their wings would not make any sound, and they were all reverently quiet. Matthew's buried soul stopped gasping out loud, but it's mouth made silent movements.

All were silent. He waited and concentrated. He listened and paid attention as he tuned in his soul ears to hear what his flesh ears could never decipher. His soul waited, and finally, Matthew's soul could hear the words of faith, seeds of wisdom, speaking to him from the ground of his heart.

Buried under mounds of negative dark words of discouragement and lies, death, and self assassination, Matthew started echoing Faith's voice from the living Words of God that were planted from years gone by. He could no longer restrain and stifle what was buried in the depths of the core of his being.

The words of life and power vibrated upward through his memory banks, and faith came flowing from Matthew's soul voice and mouth:

> Not by might, nor by power, but by my spirit, saith the Lord of hosts.
>
> Thy word have I hid in mine heart, that I might not sin against thee.
>
> My soul cleaveth unto the dust, quicken thou me according to thy word.
>
> My son, if thou wilt receive my words, and hide my commandments with thee;

So thou incline thine ear unto wisdom, and apply thine heart to understanding;

When wisdom entereth into my heart, and knowledge is pleasant unto my soul: Discretion shall preserve thee, understanding shall keep thee.

For God so loved the world, that he gave his only begotten Son, that whosoever believeth in him should not parish, but have everlasting life.

For God sent not his Son into the world to condemn the world; but that the world through him might be saved.

For the word of God is quick, and powerful, and sharper than any two-edged sword, piercing even to the dividing asunder of the soul and spirit, and the joints and marrow, and is a discerner of the thoughts and intents of the heart.

Do unto others as you would want them to do unto you.

My word is a lamp unto my feet and a light unto my path.

Greater is He that is in me than he that is in the world.

No weapon formed against me shall prosper.

God doesn't give me the spirit of fear but of power, love and a sound mind.

Turn you at my reproof: behold, I will pour out my spirit unto you, I will make known my words unto you.

The mouth of a righteous man is a well of life: but violence covereth the mouth of the wicked.

The words of a man's mouth are as deep waters, and the well spring of wisdom as a flowing brook.

Matthew could hardly keep up with the words that where flowing from the core root system of his being. From higher ground in Matthew's heartland, liquid light started trailing right into the shallow hole under the funeral tent that was set up in the valley of regret. They flowed, entered, and soaked into the concrete like soil that had been restricting Matthew's soul and holding him captive inside this open grave. The soil softened, and he could finally start to move and break his soul free and arise. It was like a dam broke within him. Rivers of living word waters flowed out of his soul's heartland soil. Parched empty wells within Matthew's heartland were being filled with the living water of God's word. Matthew's soul finally had a much-needed drink that truly quenched a thirst his flesh could never satisfy.

From just below the surface, Matthew's soul slowly climbed out of the shallow grave. It was like he came to himself. He was no longer observing from the lenses of his father's broken glasses but open-eyed and fully conscious in his second layer dimension of his being, where his mind, will, and emotions were manufacturing just below the surface of his skin, in his heartland.

CHAPTER 10

Enter In

Matthew was fully present within himself, and all attention was from his soul being. It was like his flesh had dissolved from his awareness and was no longer of any importance at the moment.

Instead of Matthew's thoughts broadcastings from the walls of his heartland, his soul spoke, "I can move, I feel unstuck! It's like the blinders have come off as soon as I got up from this confined open grave. I had no idea this was all going on inside me. This is a real place that is within me. It's a hot mess in here, but I am so glad I came on this journey. You all have helped me open another set of eyes that I really didn't know I had. I have been so confined and held captive for so long. I didn't know how to set myself free. Drinking never helped, but for small delusional moments, and when it wore off, I would feel even worse."

Addy smiled. With her sweet and humble grace, she nodded. "Your faith has set you free!"

Matthew's soul spoke again. "Yes! I found faith by speaking his word. His word is alive and full of faith and is water to my soul. It is and was good seed that was buried in me. It never expired or lost its power to produce. His word has been in me this whole time and my snotty self-willie has been responsible for this drought and three-ring circus that has been going on in me for years. I have been so blinded by my own self-willie. Dean Nile has been wearing my justification badge for when my feelings were hurt or my self-willie didn't get his way. It's like pouring gasoline on sparks that ignited my hurt and offended ego (self-willie) to fantasize and produce such a twisted private showing of doing these awful things to people. I wouldn't want this done to me. My grudges have turned my self-will into a monster that really has been only hurting me, myself, and I."

Addy lifted her hand and said, "Yes! You have found hope again and faith in his word, and now you have entered in, to help you switch your track for your train of thought. Sounds like a win-win to me!"

"Where do I go now?" Matthew's soul said.

"You still have to find where your self-willie is hiding out, and I am sure he doesn't like the light that has brightened up the place and pushed away the toxic fog that has been abiding in here," Addy said.

Matthew said, "But where do I look?"

Addy was still on Matthew's head stone in the valley of regret. "Rightly divide and think. The devil can never create, only copy and pervert. He is the father of all lies and a master deceiver. Where did man lose God-consciousness?"

Matthew's soul answered, "In the garden."

"Yes! Where did man gain self-consciousness?" Addy asked.

"In the garden, at the 'tree of knowledge of good and evil.' Wow, this is my garden in my heart. I have let self-willie turn most of it into a toxic forest in here, so I probably have a tree of 'all about *me*' in here somewhere!"

Matthew's soul had a keen alertness all of a sudden. He looked back at his tombstone, "Thank you, Addy! I think I know where that little brat of mine is!" Hope started blinking again and followed Matthew's resurrected soul. He headed back into toxic forest. They all followed him. It was still thorny and sticky in some places from the black bile that had been oozing from his heartland memory banks, but it was much easier to see now that the liquid light had dissolved the toxic fog and over powered the darkness. Matthew's soul was walking with a certainty of where he was going. Hope continued blinking with excitement and didn't want to miss a thing. Faith bees and Addy followed as his resurrected soul walked deeper into his forest.

Matthew's soul was walking like he was a parent, hot on the trail to a disobedient child in need of a much-needed trip to the wood shed and time out. Maybe more like jail time. With every step his soul took, you could see his countenance growing stronger as he started forging thru the trees and debris. As he pulled down over grown weeds, he exposed hidden childish toys, tokens, marbles, jacks, toy cars, and trucks—even one of his sister's favorite dolls, tied up with a jump rope. The further he went into the forest, the more rubble and hoarded trophy trinkets he found. It was overflowing with evidence that he was closing in on the right path that would lead him to this little monster.

Right in the center of toxic forest stood the biggest tree of all. Matthew's soul stopped and focused on a rope ladder hanging from the tree. He walked closer and started to climb up into a tree house that couldn't be seen from the forest bed. He found a door in the floor of the outside deck and climbed thru it. He stood before another door and saw a sign hanging above it, "Warehou-shhh."

Without pausing, Matthew's soul swung the door wide open with force. Addy, Faith bees, and Hope followed Matthew's soul in. It was very dim in there. The windows were covered with old towels and rags as curtains. All the passengers of self-willie's show were on the floor hiding under '60s style printed children sheets and bedding. They all peeked their heads up just enough so you could see that they had their finger over their mouths saying, "Shh, shh."

All of Dean Nile's costumes were lying scattered on the floor of the warehou-shhh. As he stood there, he saw many objects that reminded him of painful times from his past that had caused many blemishes and disfigurement to his emotions. Not just only from his childhood, but from his adult life as well. His guitar was broken in the open case, his father's broken sunglasses, chipped marbles, broken toys, his dad's dirty boots, his mother's torn sweater and some of her other clothes, broken dishes, school papers and tests, bad report cards, and invitations to parties he never got to go to. Even a bracelet and expensive hair comb that he had bought for his ex-wife was lying amongst the relics that archived his emotional suffering. There was witchcraft paraphernalia to cast his spells and voodoo onto the passengers he hated. Over in the back left corner was a platform stage with a childish constructed podium on it. Matthew's soul walked toward it.

Hiding behind the podium, sat his adolescent self-willie on the floor, holding his knees to his chest with his face buried in them. On the podium was a large constructed handmade book titled, "Self-Willie Book of Life."

Matthew's soul walked over to a somewhat camouflaged storage door that was locked behind the stage. He kicked it opened with force and stepped inside. Matthew's soul was in shock at the wonderful trinkets and reminders of joyful, tender, benevolent moments throughout his life that he had forgotten about. Or did he forget? Because this self-willie jerk had hid them from his soul's memory banks? Like a hoarder of delight, exhilaration, and love that self-willie wanted to lock away from, and starve his soul from pleasure, so he could use it for his own stingy entertainment and source of control and power.

His favorite toys, all shiny and new, as if he just opened them up from Christmas mornings or birthdays, were all stuffed away, hidden and blocked from the soul's ability to reconnect in mindful reminiscing. His "mighty mike," "varoom truck," and even one of his favorite t-shirts that he almost wore out, "the green hornet."

His favorite fishing pole and tackle box that his maternal grandfather gave him was locked away in secret storage from his memories.

There was his mother's guitar that she so lovingly gave to Matthew because his was broken. He had forgotten that he truly had a natural gift and passion for music, lyrics, and singing. Random pages of poetry and lyrics were tossed about with careless consideration, for it's soulful value that would even touch someone deeply in their spirit. Awards were lying about that were won at talent contests, and as he touched them, some of the songs began to vibrate from the walls of this concealed storage room. Thank you notes from area churches for Matthew's performances were scattered on the floor.

A gum wrapper that was attached to a memory of a pre-teen girl he had once had a crush on, touched his soul tenderly as he remembered the moment they shared this stick of gum. This allocated hidden space of the warehou-shh of treasured moments woke up his soul's ability to feel goodness and wonderful emotional vibrations that touched him deeply in soul/heart in ways that had been dormant, lost, and lifeless for many, many years.

As he picked up several still pictures, they would play out those moments *live* within the framed boarders, and even whiffs of fragrance would come forth that were attached to that memory. His special private memories of the girlfriend of his youth, that had become his wife and gave birth to their children, were all locked up and kept here, so his soul had such a hard time reconnecting emotionally to any of them. He found a small wooden cross that was attached to a long leather string that he wore as a necklace that was given to him at Heartland Church Camp the summer he gave his heart to Jesus. He saw his *rebirth* certificate that marked the date of August 15, 1966, that he became born again. The heartfelt joy of that moment came flooding back along with the rejoicing and clapping of the Heartland Church group. His soul smiled with the assurance of that earthly moment that he decided his eternal destination and that Jesus was his savior.

But on top the rubble of discarded memorabilia, he picked up his favorite quilt that his great grandmother had made for him when he was little. The memory of her came flooding back to him as he held the blanket close to his soul face. Her homemade mid-calf dress, trimmed with tatted lace that she had made, black tie-up shoes, and her beautiful white hair, neatly tied in a bun. He could even smell her in this moment. She always smelt like the freshest laundry.

He saw himself as a little boy, sitting on her lap, as she showed him the train that she had stitched onto the quilt she had made for him. He heard her sweet words echo in his heart, "Great grandma has prayed that your train will be filled with all good things!"

The memory faded, and he placed the quilt over the railing of his baby crib that was also there in this hidden storage. He looked down and saw what self-willie had been hiding under Matthew's favorite quilt. It had been covering just what Matthew's soul needed. Self-willie had been hiding it from his soul all this time. He picked up and put on the belt of truth and then strapped on the breastplate of righteousness, then slipped on the shoes of peace. He put on the helmet of salvation, and lifted up the shield of faith.

As he did so, all of the faith bees that came from God's Word (that was filled with Matthew's voice) in one magnificent orchestrated movement, they joined together like cell matter and created a mighty supernatural strength to his shield. Then he saw a bright shining beam of light that was hovering about three inches in front of his quilt, right in front of the train that she had stitched.

Matthew remembered the bright light that Addy had brought to him when he was in the tree, which rolled out as a scroll, and he read God's Word from.

A dim handle appeared at the top of the shaft of light, which turned it into the sword of the spirit. He picked it up and was ready for battle.

Matthew's soul dressed in the full armor of God, turned and headed right for his self-willie. Pointing the sword at him, Matthew's soul said, "Self-willie, you are under arrest." Self-willie was very weak, and as he looked up with fear, he raised his hands as he surrendered. "You have held me hostage long enough, now you get into jail."

As Matthew's soul spoke those words, they instantly formed into to a box shaped jail cell around self-willie. Matthew's soul walked over and locked the cell door. Self-willie was still holding his hands up as a submitted sign of surrender. There was no point of escape.

"Your Dean Nile act is over. Now you are going to meet my denial!"

Matthew's soul was walking away from the warehou-shh, up rightly and bold with the armor of God on, to a gate within his heartland called the *Potter's Field*. From this soul's side of the gate in heartland, it looked like it might be an entrance to a graveyard, but there was a wall of mist that divided and blocked the view to what was past the entrance gate.

Hope, Faith bees, and Addy followed a short distance behind him. They just observed what Matthew's soul was doing. It was like he didn't even know or care that they were still with him. Matthew's soul willingly opened the gate, and the swinging of the gate doorway caused a gentle breeze to flow from the mist side thru heartland. Matthew's soul knelt down on his right knee, rested the upright shield of faith on the ground while still holding onto it. With the other hand, he placed the pointed edge of the sword of the spirit into the ground of his heartland soil. He reverently bowed his head and submitted his soul. Out of his soul stepped his born again spirit man (wearing a floor length white robe with a sash, and purple cape). Every fiber of his spirit being, along with his clothing, was etched in light and was ready to enter in to the next dimension of his being. Crossing the threshold of the gate doorway that separated his soul realm from his spirit realm, his born again spirit man walked forward alone.

As Matthew's spirit man walked down a pathway by instinctual faith, the mist parted from his wake. His steady stride lead to steps in front of the secret place door. He slowly climbed the three steps and then put his spirit man hand on the doorknob. As he slowly opened the door, sparks of brilliant light burst out of the doorframe and filled the open doorway. The only thing that could be seen was a white wing that guided Matthew's spirit man in for private counsel. The door closed, and liquid light continued to flow out from under the doorway, down the steps, and onto the pathway that lead back to the gate entrance and crossed over to Matthew's soul heartland soil. The liquid light was turning lifeless soil into fresh new growth around his submitted soul.

Hope was beyond thrilled and shouted, "He's in! He's in! Matthew found his glimmers! I knew it to be so!" She was flying about in all directions. They all rejoiced for him!

"I see! I see!" Matthew earnestly said out loud.

He opened his eyes, and he was lying on the ground in front of the smoldering leftovers of the campfire and empty crushed beer cans tossed about. He sat up slowly and looked around for his new friends. He stood up and looked into the tree. The city was gone. As he looked further up into the tree, there hung his father's glasses. Weather worn and corroded, but there they were stuck, since Daniel Jones threw them up there in the summer of 1966.

Matthew was driving home from his unexpected encounter. It seemed so real to him or was it just a dream. How could he ever even begin to explain it to anyone? He looked at himself in the rearview mirror and ran his hand thru his hair, then noticed something was stuck to his tooth. He ran his tongue over it and then reached up and put it onto his finger to get a closer look at it. It was a piece of corn! He quickly looked at the trash that he had collected from his camp out. It was lying on the floor in front of the passenger's seat. All he saw were empty beer cans and an empty bag of chips. He still had the piece of corn on his finger. "It was real!" he said out loud to himself. He placed the piece of corn on the dashboard, right under the mirror so he could look at it again, and again to help him make sense of what maybe happening here. Matthew took one more look at the floor at all the empty beers cans. He raised his eyebrow and shook his head slightly, "I should be having quite a hang over after drinking all of that, but I have never felt better. I am not crazy!"

Matthew was smiling from ear to ear and had not felt this kind of inner peace since he couldn't remember when. He continued driving back toward his home, and along came a driver, acting like he owned the road. He pulled up next to Matthew at a stoplight and acted irritated that he had to stop too. Impatiently, the somewhat hostel mid-thirty-aged man revered his engine like it was going to help the light turn green sooner. Matthew looked at this man out of the corner of his eye and what he saw shocked him. It was a little bully boy, about eight years old, sitting within this man, holding on to the steering wheel, and pushing the peddle. The flesh man the only person in the truck was looking straight ahead, but this eight-year-old sitting in him, turned to look at Matthew, and stuck out his tongue. The light finally turned green and the man sped off.

Off in the distance, Matthew could hear a train whistle blowing, and he cracked a smile and looked back at his piece of corn he put on the dash.

CHAPTER 11

The Key

Matthew showed up carrying a covered dish (corn casserole) and a cooler full of drinks to share at the Thomas family reunion. It was taking place in one of the shelter houses at the same park that he used to swim at when he was a child. He had not been there in years. Aunt Flo spotted him and took his dish quickly and set it down for him and gave him a big long awaited hug.

"Oh, Matthew, I am so glad you decided to join us. It has been way too long!" Aunt Flo said as she was still embracing him.

"Yes, it has," Matthew said.

"So how have you been these days?" Aunt Flo said with her hand on his shoulder. "Okay, I've been working a lot of over time covering for someone who is off on bereavement. His son was in a bicycle accident," Matthew answered.

"That wouldn't happen to be Phyllis and Carl Jones's grandson would it?" Aunt Flo asked.

"Yes, yes it was. I work with their son Daniel. We used to live across the street from each other when we were kids, and we were in the same grade in school too," Matthew informed.

Aunt Flo rubbed her chin, "Hmm. Did you know a Sally Mortez? I think she was close to your age."

Matthew stroked his foot on the ground and paused for a moment. "Yes, I think she went to Heartland Church Camp when we were young."

"Oh, Sally's mother, Rosa was my best friend. Rosa just passed away a couple of weeks ago. Sally is moving into her mother's house and is also taking care of her estate. She was her only child. That girl is like a second daughter to me. She is just as wonderful and caring as her mother Rosa was." Aunt Flo's eyes were welled up with tears.

Matthew said, "I think I met Rosa once or twice at Hector's Café."

"You probably did. Hector was Rosa's brother," Aunt Flo said.

"I don't think I ever met Sally's dad though," Matthew replied.

She looked at him and said, "Yes, you have Matthew."

He shook his head and said, "No. No I don't believe I have."

Matthew looked at her with some confusion. Aunt Flo looked him straight into his eyes, "He lived right across the street from you growing up!"

"No. Carl Jones lived across the street from us."

Aunt Florence looked around to see if anyone was in earshot. "Rosa made me promise not to tell anyone, but she has paid long enough and now she is dead."

Sincerely and seriously, she quietly said, "Sally's father is Carl Jones.

Matthew was stunned. "Say what?"

"Carl and Rosa met in high school and dated secretly for two years after they graduated. They were each other's first loves. Rosa was Spanish, and Carl was afraid that she would never be accepted by his mother because of her strong prejudices. Carl knew his mother would crucify her daily if they were to get married. Things were so different back then." Aunt Flo was shaking her head and showing some relief from telling someone. Finally!

"Carl's mother always called Rosa a slut, but Carl knew that wasn't true because they were each other's first everything. Rosa loved Carl so much that she broke it off to save Carl from the wrath of his over barring mother. Carl was never the same after that. It was like part of him died when they separated. Rosa moved away and was already pregnant with Sally but never hung Carl with the blame. Rosa raised Sally on her own."

Matthew asked, "Did Carl ever find out Sally was his?"

Aunt Flo continued, "Carl was out of town on business and he bumped into Rosa three years after Sally was born. As soon as Carl laid eyes on Sally, he knew she was his. Carl wanted to help Rosa and Sally in someway, so he came to Phyllis with the truth, and she came unglued."

Sarcastically and shaking his head, "Oh man, I can only imagine!"

"Oh, Phyllis ruled Carl from that day forward with shame and guilt because she wanted it to look like she had the first love spot in Carl's life, but in reality could never have it."

Matthew said, "So that's why Phyllis didn't like Sally. She was afraid that Daniel was falling for his own half sister."

Aunt Flo said, "Yes! And that self-righteous, goody two shoes was pregnant before her and Carl were married, but Phyllis tried to tell everyone that Daniel was conceived on their honeymoon. She went around telling everyone that Daniel was premature because he was born seven months after they were married."

She was laughing, "But Daniel weight was a hefty nine pounds as a premie."

"So, her secret and her need to control another secret was her full time job!" Matthew said.

Nodding her head, Aunt Flo head said, "She couldn't handle honesty because it messed up her illusion that she was wanting everyone else to buy."

Matthew said, "Phyllis always had a need to appear perfect."

Aunt Flo said, "That women would rather live in denial than admit she ever did anything wrong." Putting her hand on Matthew's arm, she continued, "Ugh enough about that woman. I have something I have been wanting to give you for years." She dug in her purse and pulled out an envelope. "It's not much, but I think you should have this. I know my dad wanted Bruce, your dad, to have it, but he wouldn't take it."

Matthew took the envelope from her, "What is this?"

Matthew slowly opened a small manila envelope and a large key fell out into his hand with a D stamped into it.

Aunt Flo said, "It was my father's. Your grandfather, Jack, used to be a train switch operator."

Matthew just stood there stunned as he kept his eyes on the D key. "This was Jack Thomas, my grandfather's?"

Aunt Flo said, "Yes!"

Matthew look back up at her. "I never met him because he died before I was born."

Aunt Flo said, "No. That's not true, he died in the fall of 1966."

Matthew said, "Dad told us he died before my sisters and I were born."

Aunt Flo answered, "Well, my brother, Bruce, hated our dad for many reasons."

"Why?" Matthew asked.

She replied, "Jack Thomas was an alcoholic and was extremely hard on your father, Bruce. He was the oldest and the only boy. Bruce had to become the man of the house at the age of fourteen when your grandfather, Jack, went to prison. Bruce always resented him for it."

Matthew continued, "What happened that made him go to prison? Dad never said one word about him except that he was dead."

Aunt Flo, "Your grandfather, Jack, ran away from home before he was fifteen because he didn't want to work on the farm anymore. Jack didn't get along with his own father either. He ended up working for the railroad. Jack, our father, was mean and took his anger out on everybody."

Matthew looked back at the key in his hand and said, "Sounds just like my dad, Bruce."

Sincerely, Aunt Flo said, "I am truly sorry about that Matthew, but there was no reaching Bruce on this issue."

"No kidding!" Matthew replied.

"Your grandfather, Jack, used to lay new rails for a new track that they were putting in, and then later became a train switch operator. Back in the day, they used to use Morse code to get their instructions on when to switch the tracks. Well, Jack was drinking on the job one night and missed the communication to switch the track. This caused a train full of coal to hit a passenger train head on. Both trains derailed and the two engineers were killed. Thank God that the passenger train had just dropped off the passengers before the accident happened or their would have been more fatalities."

Matthew said, "Oh my gosh, that must have been horrible to bare."

Aunt Flo continued, "Your grandfather was sent to prison for life. Of course this forced him to sober up. He tried writing to your father over the years, but Bruce would never open any of the them."

Matthew had a sudden reaction, "Oh my gosh!"

"What is it, Matthew?" she said.

"I forgot something!" He reached over to her and gave her another big hug. "Thank you so much for telling me this. I have got to go do something that I forgot about. It is really important. Can I call you?"

"Sure thing! I would love that, Matthew!" she said.

She waved as she watched him run back to his truck. As soon as Matthew pulled into his own driveway, he shut off his truck, hopped out, and started looking quickly thru his key ring for the key to unlock his work van. "Come on!" he said to himself. He finally found it and went right to the back door of the van and started looking for his tool belt. He grabbed it and pulled out the envelope that he had stuffed into his tool belt when he was in the attic of his childhood home.

Matthew's heart was pounding, so he sat down on the floorboard of his van with the doors open. He examined the unopened, aged, and soiled envelope from when his younger self hid it under his rug in his bedroom and spilled grape juice on it before church camp in 1966.

Matthew slowly ran his finger over the envelope and realized that this was the only thing that he had, other than the key that Aunt Flo had given him, that was straight from his grandfather—like DNA touching DNA. With a small stroked force from his fingernail, it was easy to open the still sealed envelope, and it was never opened by his father, Bruce. He pulled out the paper and carefully unfolded the letter Jack (his grandfather) wrote from prison.

August 8, 1966
Dear Bruce,

This will be the last letter that I will ever write you. I understand that you want nothing to do with me, and I do not hold that against you or blame you in any way. I am not well, and I want you to know that I am not afraid to die. I have found hope and faith, which opened my eyes to insight that helped me see things that only God's word could show me. I have made my peace with God, and to the best of my ability, the families of the two engineers that lost their lives in the accident I caused. But what I am most sorry for is what I have done to you. I was angry and bitter at my own childhood, and I passed that pain onto my own children, especially you, my only son. I know my drinking has destroyed and caused so much pain for so many innocent souls. I have been very selfish in my actions, and for that I am truly sorry. Please forgive me. God's word and his everlasting grace has changed my heart.

You may not believe it, but I know it to be so!

I love you, Dad.

Jack Thomas

Tears were running down Matthew's face, and his mind was racing and trying to make connections with the evidence before him. From the anger of Jack's father all the way through to Matthew—that's four generations. Why did this divine event happen to him at the tree?

"What am I supposed to do with all of this? Why me? Why now? Rightly divide, rightly divide. I am a three-part being—body, soul, and spirit." Matthew said under his breath. He started breathing in and out, and closing his eyes to regroup.

That last work order of Daniel's, was that a gift? What if he had never gone back to his childhood home? What if he had never gone back to Heartland camp? What if he had never found hope and faith at the tree? What if he had not gone to the reunion? Was the D key that Aunt Flo gave him a gift or puzzle piece too?

Matthew noticed that the grape juice stain that he caused when he was a young boy had soaked through his bedroom rug onto the envelope and onto the letter. As he held it up to the light, he could see the shape of a heart on the letter. Right in the center of the heart was a fold that made it appear to be a broken heart, but in that centerfold line were the words, "I know it to be so!"

Matthew began to weep.

CHAPTER 12

Food for Thought

Matthew was standing in front of his living room window, looking out at the trash cans that Danny Junior used to knock over. How his thought life has been altered since that boy's funeral. Then he stepped away and noticed the old family Bible that was on the shelf and grabbed it and finally opened it up.

As he did, the pages flopped opened to a passage, and Matthew started reading it out loud to himself, "For though we walk in the flesh, we do not war after the flesh. (For the weapons of our warfare are not carnal, but mighty through God to the pulling down of strongholds). Casting down imaginations, and every high thing that exalteth itself against the knowledge of God, and bringing into captivity every thought to the obedience of Christ."

Matthew sat down in his favorite chair in the living room and stared at his father's weather worn corroded sunglasses that had hung in the tree for most of his life. Lying next to the glasses in front of him was the train switch D key from his grandfather that his Aunt Flo had given him and an unopened beer bottle. They were all displayed before him on the coffee table. He picked up the bottle and looked at the word, "beer." As he held the bottle in his hand, he moved his thumb and covered the letter R, which made him see the word, "bee," instead of beer. Faith instantly flooded his mind and thoughts. *I need a drink of faith, not beer.* Matthew breathed out loud to himself as if he was voicing something to his internal committee. He sat the beer bottle down.

"Rightly divide, Matthew. Rightly divide." He reached for the D key and held it in his hand. He took one more look at his father's glasses and closed his flesh eyes.

He was holding and rubbing the train switch key.

Darkness was all around, and the only thing that was heard was a key jingling on a large key ring. Matthew's soul was walking along a dimly lit pathway dressed in the full armor of God and the more steps that he took the brighter the pathway became. Hooked onto his belt of truth was the D key. He unhooked it, and he looked over to his left shoulder at a jail cell with a figure that had his back to him. He was dressed like an inmate. He slowly rotated around on the stool to face Matthew's soul. It was Matthew's adolescent self-willie looking very weak and disturbed. He was glaring at him with hatred, and self-willie was not happy having to submit to rules that confined him. Matthew's soul took a look around at his heartland and noticed a difference in the landscape. It still was a mess, but he noticed more light and new growth. Faith bees were at work cross-pollinating and new life was popping up everywhere producing good food for thought. The more of God's word that Matthew spoke out loud to himself, gave more faith and seeds of wisdom to be sown and planted, which caused more cross pollination to occur and materialize within.

Faith bees were covered in tiny sprinkles of light pollen, and as they landed on the jail cell, some of that light pollen would drop off of them. They continued going about their business and doing what they were designed to do and would leave behind bee-leavens for self-willie to sample when he got hungry. This was all that self-willie had on his menu. Something so different and unusual for him to digest and think about, taste, and see that it was sweet and good for the soul and even for the bones. Matthew paid no attention to self-willie, and went about his business. Matthew's soul walked over to a storage box that was buried in a shallow ditch bank in his heartland. He took the D key and opened the deposit box, and inside was his father's belt and a word capsule (like the one in the drive thru bank) full of black hateful, curses, and distorted word currency that had been deposited from the three generations of men before him.

As Matthew's soul lifted the belt out if the box, self-willie yelled, "Oh, the belt we were beaten with, remember?"

Matthew's soul said nothing. Summer of 1966, flash back memory.

Matthew opened his bedroom door, dove onto his bedroom floor rug and quickly crawled under the bed. "Matthew!" Bruce, his dad yelled.

Matthew was holding as still as he possibly could while his father, Bruce, stepped into his bedroom to see if he was there. Then his dad went to check the bathroom, and Matthew came out from under the bed and ran to the basement. In the background, he could still hear Bruce yelling.

Matthew was hiding underneath the steps, and a few moments later, he could hear his father's footsteps, coming down the stairs, and he could see his dad's boots through a large knothole in the underside of the stair board. "You better tell me, boy. Where are my sunglasses?" Bruce stepped into the storage room under the steps and pulled the chain to turn the light on. Matthew was hiding under the steps, and Bruce pulled off his belt. "Please, Daddy. Don't! No! No!" Matthew pleaded.

Matthew's soul picked up the belt, the word currency container, and started walking. Self-willie yelled, "Look at our blood stain still on the belt and the buckle. It's our blood, Matthew. He cut us deep. We have a scar to prove it." Stopping along the path, Matthew's soul took his right foot and kicked away some dead lifeless rubble and pulled a few vines off of a shaft, and underneath it was a train switch.

"We had to get stitches for it! We lied to the doctor and told him we fell out of a tree just to cover his ass," Self-willie continued yelling.

Matthew's soul inserted the D key into the keyhole. He pulled the lever, switched the track, and started walking again. He walked up to an empty old rail car, opened the side door, climbed into it, and then closed the door behind him. Matthew's soul tossed the belt onto the floor of the railcar. He opened the word capsule full of black matter word currency that had been passed down to him by his father,

Bruce; grandfather, Jack Thomas; and his great grandfather, Frank Thomas. As he tossed the black matter word currency onto the floor of the train car, it expanded and filled the entire car almost to over flowing. It looked like black coal. Matthew's soul stepped through a small door in the front of the car that was next to the train engine.

He grabbed a shovel that was hanging on the wall at the front of the car and started to shovel the black matter word currency one scoop at a time into the engine of the train. It sparked, lit up in the engine, and started to burn hotter with each shovel full. The train made loud, racking, jolting noises like it had not moved because of so much rust and decay, but slowly, it started in a forward motion. Matthew's soul began to shovel faster and faster, and with every load, he tossed into the fire and he said, "I forgive them! I forgive them!"

As the front grill of the engine passed the switch that was just turned in the track—the muck, rusty crust, and decay started to fall off the old train of thought, transforming it into a glorious train made of precious metals and gold, adorn with jewels and diamonds.

Self-willie was in shock at the new train of thought that appeared before him. He had never produced or conducted something so wonderful as this. Self-willie was now standing up with his hands on the cell bars straining to see what was happening.

Matthew's soul found the tree of me and told everyone that they were free to go, and board the new train of thought. "I am sorry and I forgive you. You do not belong here anymore!"

Every character and previous hostage had stunned looks on their faces and were truly thankful for their freedom pass. He threw out all the garbage from the warehous-shh and put it in the hole under the tent in the valley of regret. As he stepped back from the hole in the ground that his soul once was stuck in, he covered it up, and said, "It's about time I took out the real trash!"

Self-willie was watching what Matthew's soul had done to the tree of me.

Matthew's soul walked over to the gate called the Potter's Field that divided the soul realm from the spirit realm. He knelt down once again and submitted his soul, and his spirit man stepped out of his soul and walked through the gate alone toward the *secret place* for private counsel.

Self-willie said nothing as he stared through the bars on his cell wondering what might be beyond the Potter's Field Gate, but at that moment, he looked down at the light pollen that was stuck to his hands. He rotated both hands and was mesmerized at this new beautiful item he had not seem before. Self-willie slowly stuck out his tongue to taste it. His face totally changed its continence as the sweetness melted upon his tongue. "Hey, this is good! Bee-leavens is Good!"

Matthew opened his eyes and smiled to himself. He finally took the time to focus on what he had gleaned from his tree encounter. He looked at his father's old sunglasses once again as they were still on the coffee table before him. He really noticed the difference this time as he picked them up. They had no sting attached to them.

Matthew's soul had no longer listened to his self-willie rants but started doing his soul works that faith could not do. Taking control of self-willie and letting his spirit man guide him with the wisdom he gathered from the private counsel he received in the secret place. Self-willie no longer had a seat or access to Matthew's control panel. He was not the conductor of the train of thought or the producer and server of food for thought.

Garbage in your thought life, garbage out of your mouth, and toxic seeds sown to produce your defeated earth life that leads you to a dammed eternity that you chose yourself by doing it your way! Just like the souls that dwell in the people who sit in jail cells in the natural, they don't get a choice about what is being served. Matthew started to notice that his internal thermostat that is wired to his emotions and temper were starting to change. The entrance of Words of God's wisdom were changing his lack of understanding and was bringing assurance and an inner calmness that he never had before he invited Hope and Faith to come in. God-consciousness was returning and self-willie's tree of me was being pruned by Matthew's soul as his spirit man instructed him to do.

Later that afternoon, Matthew decided to go for a drive, and he pulled into the gated graveyard that he had first heard the loud buzzing of the mysterious bee that visited him twice by Danny Junior's grave side tent. He found comfort in knowing that his coworker, Sam, heard and saw the bee too that day. He drove by Danny's grave and moved on to the next few sections of grave plots. He pulled up his truck and parked at that familiar area where the stone of Bruce Thomas was located.

He stood before his father's head stone for a long silent moment and then placed his father's sun glasses upon the sill below his engraved name. Matthew bent down, laid his hand upon his father's stone, and said, "Even if you never said you were sorry to me, or my mother and sisters, I forgive you!"

Matthew stood back up and said, "This curse is broken!"

As Matthew started walking back to his truck, he heard someone call out his name from the next section over.

"Matthew?" He turned toward the voice.

"Matthew Thomas?" He nodded his head yes.

"It's Sally. Sally Mortez." She walked over to him and greeted him with a friendly handshake. "Wow, it's been a long time?" She looked down at the Bruce Thomas's head stone and said, "Are those your dad's glasses from Heartland Church Camp?"

Matthew looked at her and did a small laugh. "Yep, I finally gave them back!"

CHAPTER 13

The Heart Sings

Matthew was in his bedroom, and he started to remove a few things that had been stacked upon the top of his guitar case, along with the dust that had built up. He grabbed a dirty old t-shirt and finished off the rest of the dust cloud on the case and slowly opened it. Just like Sally, it was like seeing an old friend again. He put brand new strings on the guitar and started to tune it up. Matthew noticed that he seemed to be more in touch with his feelings, but they were not ruling him any longer. Something was changing in his core. It was free—a freedom and liberation that he had never known before. He was awake in his triune being. He was discovering new ideas and imaginations that were coming forth from within. He started strumming and reconnecting with his guitar and humming a few bars that had just arrived from deep within him…

One year later…

There was a full house this evening at Hector's Café. There had been remodeling done with a whole huge addition built on for banquets, wedding receptions, conferences, open mike night, karaoke, and live music. Sally walked up to Matthew, rubbed his shoulders, and gave him a friendly kiss on the cheek. "You will do great!" Matthew slowly walked up to the small stage, sat down on a stool with his guitar, and adjusted the microphone.

Matthew cleared his throat, "I would like to thank everyone who came out to night, to help dedicate this new addition to Hector's Café in the loving memory of his sister, Rosa, also Sally's mother."

As Matthew looked out at the crowd, he noticed it was packed up to fire code, and they even had to open the patio section as well. Several coworkers and friends were scattered around the room. Matthew centered himself, closed his eyes for a brief moment, wanted to stop the feeling of being self-conscious, and tuned himself into being God-conscious.

Matthew spoke. "I would like to share tonight a song that I wrote a few months ago called I Know It To Be So!"

A few months later...

Phyllis Jones was driving her car, listening to the radio, and she found that she was really enjoying a song, then the radio announcer said, "That was written and sung by a new local artist, Matthew Thomas!"

Phyllis started to freak out and instantly shut off her radio.

"Oh. No way! Not that little jerk who was always picking on my precious son."

She was interrupted by a loud train horn. *Woo Hoo!* She slammed on her breaks as she ran the front of her car into the railroad-crossing arm. She smacked her head on the horn of the steering wheel. Her wig and glasses were all messed up, and she began honking the horn hysterically at the train.

Phyllis had her window down, and a bee was sitting on her outside rear view mirror. As Phyllis reset her wig back straight on her head and tried to adjust her glasses, that bee winked before it buzzed right on into Phyllis's car. Phyllis's snobby adolescent self-willie, sitting inside of her body, dressed in her Sunday clothes and white gloves, started screaming wildly and swatting.

The end!

A beautiful little lightning bug came flying by and popped the *end* word and turned it into the *bee-ginning*!

ABOUT THE AUTHOR

Born and raised in Ohio and just out of high school, Connie wanted to know if God could hear her. She sent out a test signal and when she least expected it, he answered. Then began the classroom of life. Connie got married, had a son, and her parents divorced shortly thereafter.

All within the next five years, four pillar family members died and one was her mother. Less then ten months after burying her, she had a daughter; six and a half months later, her father died; in less than nine months following, she gave birth to another daughter.

Her heart was broken with grief and pain, but mixed with the joy of new children. They moved back into her childhood home for ten years where only she could see and hear the dreadful echoes of the past, but everyone else that lived there was free.

During those years she was a stay at-home mom, and the Holy Spirit guided her into her own heart/soul for some renovations and cross pollinated her thinking with God's word.

They built a new home, and twelve years later, they divorced after twenty-eight years of unresolvable core value differences.

This story came alive in her imagination and dreams, for over twenty years, it would not leave Connie alone. God pointed out to her that what she hated most was her assignment and problem to solve.

She entered in, went back to her pain, and found where her treasure was.

Her prayer is that she hopes it to be so for you too!

She is happily remarried, living in Tennessee.

Printed in the USA
CPSIA information can be obtained
at www.ICGtesting.com
CBHW031323171123
1934CB00001B/12